Library of Congress Cataloging-in-Publication Data available.
ISBN 978-1-4521-0917-6

Book design by Eloise Leigh and Mark Neely.
Typeset in Akzidenz-Grotesk Std.

Manufactured in China.

10 9 8 7 6 5 4 3 2 1

Chronicle Books LLC
680 Second Street, San Francisco, California 94107
www.chroniclekids.com

Visit **www.worstcasescenarios.com** to learn more about the series.

Image credits: Page 187: (nautical chart and compass) Moth/Dreamstime.com; (tablet) Jirkacafa/Dreamstime.com; (wood background and note papers) Grafvision/Dreamstime .com; (watch) Defun/Dreamstime.com. Page 188: (compass) Moth/Dreamstime.com. Page 190: (wood background and note papers) Grafvision/Dreamstime.com; Page 193: (bowline knot) Pancaketom/Dreamstime.com; (reef knot) Porbeagle/Dreamstime.com; (round turn and two half-hitches knot) digitalreflections/Shutterstock.com; (wood background and note papers) Grafvision/Dreamstime.com. Page 195: (compass) Zhuanghua/Dreamstime.com; (great white shark) Puddingpie/Dreamstime.com; (shark inset) Thediver123/Dreamstime .com; (tablet) Jirkacafa/Dreamstime.com; (wood background and note papers) Grafvision/ Dreamstime.com. Page 196: (Panama Canal) Chris Jenner/Shutterstock.com. Page 197: (nautical chart and compass) Moth/Dreamstime.com; (tablet) Jirkacafa/Dreamstime .com; (wood background and note papers). Page 198: (box jellyfish) Pniesen/Dreamstime .com; (puffer fish, lionfish) Lilithlita/Dreamstime.com; (wood background and note papers) Grafvision/Dreamstime.com.

The
WORST-CASE SCENARIO

AN ULTIMATE ADVENTURE NOVEL

DEADLY SEAS

YOU DECIDE HOW TO SURVIVE!

By David Borgenicht and Alexander Lurie
with Mike Perham, sailing consultant

Illustrated by Yancey Labat

chronicle books · san francisco

WELCOME TO YOUR
DEADLY SEAS ADVENTURE

WHAT WILL YOU DO?

ONE WRONG MOVE COULD SPELL DISASTER.

YOU and five crew members are going to sail around the world! It will be the ultimate challenge of your bravery and endurance. You'll face dangers you never imagined. Not many people have accomplished this daring feat. Will you become one of the few to battle the wild seas and win?

At many points in this fantastic adventure, you'll be given choices—and the decisions you make will change the course of your story.

◀━┫ *It's all up to you.* ┣━▶

There are thirty-three possible endings to your Deadly Seas adventure. But there is only ONE PATH through the book that will take you around the world on your first try.

Before you start, make sure to read the Expedition File at the back of the book, beginning on page 187. It has the tips and information you'll need to make good choices.

You and the crew will work together, but ultimately, some critical decisions will come down to you. Just use your common sense and excellent judgment—and the photographers and reporters will be waiting for you on the dock to announce your victory!

THE CREW

CAPTAIN

JASON HARRINGTON
AGE: 16
HOME: LOS ANGELES, CALIFORNIA

Jason is the most experienced sailor on your yacht. In fact, he has never lived on land. He has lived on a boat his entire life. His parents joke that he learned how to tie a bowline before he could knot his own shoelaces. Jason likes being top dog and in charge. He's handsome, smart, and very sure of himself, which isn't always a good thing. Sometimes he doesn't listen to the opinions of others when it could be important. Jason thinks he's always right, and if Jason thinks so, it must be true.

BRANDON GREENE
AGE: 16 HOME: SAN DIEGO, CALIFORNIA

Brandon loves to fish and to cook his catch. But his real talent is navigating. He's great at avoiding hazards and reaching destinations on time. Brandon is a perfectionist when it comes to his navigational charts, but he's a disaster when it comes to practically everything else. He drops his stuff wherever; he'll eat whatever, whenever (and that includes moldy bread and rotten fruit). But he'll give you the shirt off his back—that is, as soon as he can find it.

CREW

CHELSEA VEGA
AGE: 15 HOME: CAPE COD, MASSACHUSETTS

Chelsea comes from a large family. She has three brothers and two sisters, and they all grew up sailing on Cape Cod. Chelsea is a natural athlete and a junior champion gymnast. She can shimmy up a yacht's mast in record time to fix sails. For fun, she climbs up blindfolded. She loves a challenge—maybe a little bit too much. Where danger looms, Chelsea follows.

CREW

CREW

CREW

DAVID LEE
AGE: 15 HOME: CHAPEL HILL, NORTH CAROLINA

David's parents are both professors of environmental studies at Duke University. His family has a house on the Outer Banks, where they go sailing whenever weather permits. David has a natural aptitude for fixing things. When he was six years old, he took apart the washing machine and used the pieces to make a miniature Ferris wheel. David will be the mechanic on this trip. He is tidy and organized, but is somewhat of a safety freak. David is also a fanatic about helping endangered species.

GEORGINA FORTUNATO
AGE: 15 HOME: MIAMI, FLORIDA

Georgina is outgoing and fun-loving. She has two passions—sailing and meteorology. She can predict foul weather with great precision and will be the yacht's weather expert. Georgina is a certified junior lifeguard. But at times her behavior is a little strange. Why won't she let Chelsea clip her nails? Why does she throw Jason's duffel overboard? Why won't she let Brandon eat a banana? A sneak peek into her diary will reveal all.

THE ADVENTURE BEGINS . . .

"Today your life will change forever," Mr. Jules Houseman Jr. says. He is standing near the bow on the *Chronos II*, the fantastic 40-foot sailing yacht that is about to take you on a trip you'll never forget.

Mr. Houseman owns the *Chronos II* and is sponsoring your voyage for publicity—to increase sales of his world-famous watch company, Chronos.

"Today you will start your journey around the world. And you will be one of the youngest crews to do it—if you succeed." As he says this last part, he stares right at you. Then he moves to shake hands with each member of your crew.

"Welcome aboard—on your Deadly Seas adventure," he says.

You are an expert when it comes to boat handling, but your heart starts to pound anyway. You know you'll be talking about this trip for years to come—if you make it back alive . . .

CHRONOS II

You shield your eyes from the bright California sun, searching the crowd for your friends and family gathered on the Marina del Rey pier. They stand five deep along the green railing, taking photos and shouting cheers.

Next to you, Jason Harrington, the skipper of your yacht, waves to some friends. You are both experienced sailors, but Jason grew up on a boat. *He'll be a great skipper*, you think.

You've never actually met the crew before, but you're sure they'll all be terrific. They've been handpicked by Houseman for their sailing skills. Houseman selected you because you're exceptional at controlling the force of the wind on the sails.

"When do we leave? I'm ready. I wish Houseman would hurry up," Chelsea Vega says. Chelsea is totally energized. Even standing still, she seems to be in motion. She's from Cape Cod, Massachusetts, and her entire family—three brothers, two sisters, and her mom and dad—have all flown here to see her off. But Chelsea isn't really looking at them. Her bright-green eyes steal a sideways glance at Jason.

Across from you, Brandon Greene and David Lee are talking to each other. Brandon is smiling and looks relaxed. Not David. He stands stiffly, his brow lined with worry.

Brandon's long, messy brown hair falls into his eyes as he tries to read the piece of paper David is holding. He's at least a foot taller than David and he has to lean over to read. You notice that Brandon's shirt is on backward, and you wonder if he meant to wear it that way.

David's serious gaze scans the yacht. "I hope they gave us two satellite phones," he says. "It's crucial to have a backup."

You feel a tap on your shoulder. It's Georgina Fortunato, the final member of the crew.

"What a perfect day for sailing," she says. "Feel that breeze! Are we lucky or what?" Georgina's tanned face breaks into a huge smile.

"Listen up, *Chronos* crew." Mr. Houseman gets your attention. "Time to review the rules of the challenge."

You all turn to face him.

"But first, I have some bad news for you…"

"One of your satellite phones is missing . . ." he starts. All the blood drains from David's face.

"But that's no excuse. The race must go on." Houseman takes a piece of paper from his suit pocket and begins to read.

"You have 285 days to sail around the world. Come home even one day later, and you lose the challenge. All the crew members must make it back to the finish line. If someone drops out, you lose. You can use only sail power to make your trip—no engine power, no matter what. Or you lose."

"Cheerful guy," Brandon says to David. "Sounds like he doesn't want to give up the prize money."

It does sound that way, you think. But you know the real reason behind Houseman's gloomy presentation. He wants to make the rules clear—because he wants this crew to win badly.

"To officially circumnavigate the world, you must travel at least 21,600 nautical miles. You must cross the equator. And you must finish at the same port you started from," Houseman says.

"Six of you will sail off today." His gaze travels over each one of you. "And all six must return on this ship alive to win the prize money—one million dollars."

"Listen up." At the mention of the prize money, Jason springs into action. "It's time to make our final check," he says.

He orders Brandon to inspect the navigation equipment. "Make sure you have all your charts," he reminds him.

You can't be sure, but it looks as if Brandon is rolling his eyes as he heads below.

Jason tells you to check the safety devices—life jackets, flares, fire extinguishers.

"David, inspect the electronic autopilot and the hull fittings one more time."

David is on it before Jason even finishes his sentence.

"Georgina, check the food and medical supplies," Jason says as he and Chelsea walk off together to examine the rigging.

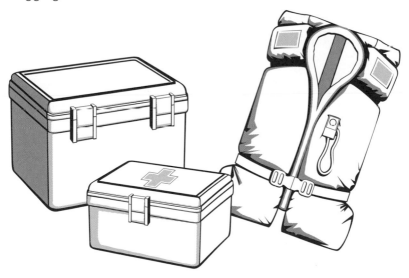

You complete your check. All emergency gear and safety devices are in good order. You see Jason and Chelsea at the helm, but before you head over, you scan the yacht from bow to stern. The *Chronos II* is beautiful. Her polished deck gleams in the sunshine. Houseman has given you an incredible boat. You can't wait to ride the waves with her.

You join Jason and Chelsea.

"One million dollars," Jason says as you approach. "I'm going to put my share of the winnings toward a new boat."

"How can you be so sure we're going to win?" Chelsea laughs.

"I've made this trip a thousand times in my mind," Jason says. "This contest is as good as won."

He turns to you. "What are you going to do with your money?"

You smile and shrug your shoulders. The truth is, the prize money isn't important to you. That's not why you took this challenge.

David, Brandon, and Georgina meet you on deck.

"We're ready to set sail," Jason reports to Mr. Houseman.

Mr. Houseman nervously runs his fingers through his thinning hair.

"The dude looks tense," Brandon whispers to you. "Not a confidence builder."

Houseman is definitely anxious, and you know why. "Crew of the *Chronos II*, I salute you." Houseman gives an awkward two-finger salute.

It's finally time to leave. You take a deep breath. The water is where you feel most at home. You can't wait to start.

"Cast off the lines," Jason tells David and Brandon.

Chelsea is holding the forward spring line—the final line to be untied.

The crowd starts to wave and cheer.

Georgina's brother rushes up to the boat. He hugs his sister and says, "Good luck!"

Georgina looks horrified and punches him in the nose. Her brother just laughs.

Weird, you think. Months later, you'll learn what that was all about.

The yacht swings away from the pier and you help Chelsea untie the final line. Jason steers away from the dock.

But there's a boat just ahead of you, leaving the harbor. Suddenly, it stops dead and throws its engine in reverse. It's moving backward now. It's going to slam right into you!

"Watch out!" David yells at the other boat. But the warning is too late.

Your dream of sailing around the world is about to come to an instant end.

But Jason steers around the boat on its leeward side and glides past it with inches to spare. He's saved the dream—for now.

⚓

As you sail toward Hawaii, the weather is great. The yacht soars over each rolling wave, skimming forward.

"Want to take the helm for a while?" Jason asks you. "I'm starving."

You jump at the chance and grab the wheel. The bow dips into the waves and sends up a shower of water. Suddenly you're soaked, but you love it.

Georgina joins you at the helm. She's a great meteorologist. Sometimes it seems as if she can tell a change in weather just by sniffing the air.

"I can't believe we're really going around the world," she says. "I just can't believe it!"

You laugh. "What's the latest forecast?"

"I just checked the computer," she says. "It looks like a small storm is headed our way. Small but powerful."

You've weathered storms before. But you feel wobbly. You don't have your sea legs yet.

The wind picks up.

The sea turns choppy.

You're at the wheel now, so it's up to you to pull the boat through her first storm. Can you do it?

Dark clouds roll in. A chill creeps into the air and you shiver. The boat begins to rock in the churning water.

Chelsea and Brandon take down the mainsail.

"It's getting rough. Better put on your safety harnesses," Jason yells up to all of you.

Whenever you're on deck you're supposed to wear the harness. It's a belt that fastens around your chest and shoulders. A sturdy tether connects it to a cable that runs the length of the boat, so you won't fall overboard.

"She's not wearing her harness." Georgina points to Chelsea. "She thinks because she's a gymnast she can somersault her way out of danger," Georgina jokes, but there's an edge to her voice.

CHRONOS II

You look through your binoculars and see a dark sheet of rain approaching.

The wind whips your face. The ship starts rocketing off the tops of the waves. This squall is a strong one. The seawater crashes in and pounds the deck.

Your feet and pants are instantly soaked.

As the waves pummel the boat, your stomach ties itself into a giant knot. The ship is handling the storm well. You wish you could say the same for yourself.

There's a tap on your shoulder. "I'll take over from here," Jason says.

You hate to admit it, but you're relieved.

Georgina and Chelsea are below, securing all loose items as the ship rocks violently back and forth.

David makes sure everything on deck is tied down tight.

Jason yells to you and Brandon over the roar of the waves, "Unfurl the staysail and foresail." These smaller sails will give Jason more control over the yacht in the strong winds.

As you and Brandon work together, you notice he doesn't look well. "Are you okay?" you ask him.

"Sure," he says, but you don't believe him. You can tell that something is wrong.

"Don't worry," you try to reassure him—and yourself, too. "The *Chronos II* is a great boat. She can handle this."

"I know," he says. "But what do you think happened to the *Chronos I*?"

"It sunk," you tell him. The words tumble out before you can stop.

Brandon looks really awful now. More frightened than ever.

"It wasn't a good yacht. Not like this one," you say—and the mast on your boat lets out a terrible groan.

Brandon's knuckles turn white as he clutches the railing. "What happened to the crew?" he asks.

"Drowned. All of them." You should have lied, you realize too late.

Brandon grips the railing tighter.

Your hands start to tremble. The rain whips your face and you can't see what you're doing.

"How do you know so much about the *Chronos I*?" Brandon asks as you finally manage to tie the sail.

You'll tell him, but not now—because he looks like he's about to pass out.

"I don't feel well," he finally admits. "I think I'm seasick. What should I do?"

IF YOU TELL BRANDON TO STAY ON DECK, TURN TO PAGE 150.

IF YOU TELL BRANDON TO GO BELOW,
TURN TO PAGE 183.

Urine? Seriously? you think. You try to protest, but Brandon convinces everyone it's the way to go.

Brandon hovers over you with a plastic cup of yellow urine. The only way you'll forgive the crew for choosing this disgusting option is if it works.

The warm liquid is poured onto the tentacles stuck fast to your leg.

Your pain surges even higher than before.

When the urine hits the tentacles, it triggers stinging cells that hadn't yet fired, causing them to inject even more venom into your skin. The venom works its way deep into your body tissue and your blood. The toxin attacks your skin, your nervous system, and then your heart.

Urine was the wrong choice. It makes the deadly tentacles inject you with even more venom. In minutes, you have a heart attack, and your life, as you knew it, is flushed away.

THE END

There's not a second to spare. You need to tighten the backstay now or the mast will break and the yacht will flip. You shudder at the thought of being flung into the churning sea. The cold water will surely kill you.

But the safety harness must wait. The sails come first.

You hurry to help Chelsea pull the wire that leads from the top of the mast to the stern of the boat. The wind slaps your face, stinging your windburned skin. The ocean spray makes it nearly impossible to see. Planting your feet as solidly as you can on the slippery deck, you heave with all your might.

The mast bends slightly, but not enough to break. As hard as you and Chelsea pull, the gale-force winds push harder in the opposite direction. It's the two of you against Mother Nature.

"Again!" you cry. Chelsea nods. The wind swirls and howls. You pull and pull. Your muscles tense and sweat mixes with sea and rainwater on your skin.

"Secure the wire!" Chelsea screams over the roar of the storm. "It's in a good position."

At that moment, the wire slips from your grip, and then you hear an awful sound.

"That loud noise was thunder, right?" you ask uncertainly. You raise your head to the sky. Rain pounds down.

"No!" Chelsea lets out a high-pitched wail. "The mast! Look! It snapped!"

You gape and squint, trying to see the extent of the damage. Through the curtains of rain, you watch the huge pole made from carbon fiber wobble in the wind. *Not good,* you think. *Not good at all.* You've had plenty of rigging problems before, but never a broken mast.

"It's coming down!" you yell suddenly.

Chelsea doesn't answer. She stands frozen, a statue in the storm, her gaze transfixed on the swaying mast. For the first time since meeting her, you see fear in Chelsea's eyes. That really scares you.

At that moment, another gust of wind sweeps across the boat. The cracked mast lets out a final groan and begins to fall. "Chelsea!" You grab her shoulders and give her a shake. "Move! Now!" you scream, fighting to be heard. You both will be crushed if the mast smashes onto the deck. You grab Chelsea's hand. Which way should you and Chelsea run? You have less than a second to decide!

IF YOU RUN TO THE BOW, TURN TO PAGE 96.

IF YOU RUN TO THE STERN, TURN TO PAGE 169.

"Water is pouring in too fast," you argue. "We *all* need to leave!"

Jason and David protest, but you hold your ground. You know Jason's upset—abandoning the boat means losing the challenge. But this isn't about winning anymore—it's about staying alive! Soon David agrees that the crack can't be repaired out at sea and especially not in a storm at night. You must get off the boat before it goes down.

Everyone rushes onto the deck. While Brandon, Chelsea, and Georgina untie the life raft, Jason does a head count. "Where's David?" he demands.

You turn back and peek below deck. "Mayday! Mayday!" you hear David repeat into the emergency radio. "This is *Chronos II-Chronos II-Chronos II* WA720."

"He's sending a distress signal!" you call back to Jason.

You scan the vast ocean. Nothing but churning water. In minutes, your raft will be bobbing all alone out there. You hope that someone hears the distress call.

The boat lurches heavily, submerging most of the starboard side. "We need to leave now!" Jason yells.

The others are already lifting the life raft into the dark ocean.

"Wait!" David calls. He is starting to relay longitude and latitude coordinates. A rescue boat or helicopter will need these to find you.

Another wave pushes the *Chronos II* inches from resting completely on its side.

"David, we're going over!" Jason bellows.

David scrambles up onto the deck. "I didn't finish," he pants. "I should go back and call—"

"You'll die down there!" You grab his arm and push him into the life raft before he can argue. Chelsea, Georgina, and Brandon are already in. The rip cord attaching the life raft to the yacht suddenly breaks free. Jason lunges for the raft and clutches it with both hands as the waves threaten to pull it out to sea and drag him along with it.

"The supplies! Get them!" Jason glances back. There's a big plastic bag with life jackets, rope, and flashlights, and there's the prepacked waterproof grab bag.

You can carry only one bag. Which one will it be?

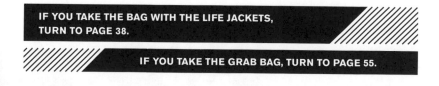

IF YOU TAKE THE BAG WITH THE LIFE JACKETS, TURN TO PAGE 38.

IF YOU TAKE THE GRAB BAG, TURN TO PAGE 55.

That green dot could mean big trouble out there. Indecision is the cause of many boating accidents, so you spring into action. You race up to the deck to search for Brandon.

"What's wrong?" Jason asks before you can find him.

"I saw something on the radar screen," you yell over the crashing waves and wind. "I don't know what it is, but it's somewhere over there." You point out the direction.

Jason peers through his high-power binoculars. "Iceberg!" he shouts. He struggles to steer the boat clear of the iceberg. But it seems hopeless. The wind is too strong to fight.

You and the crew watch in horror as the boat slams against the waves, heading right for the iceberg. Then, suddenly, the squall ends. Jason moves fast. He takes advantage of the new conditions and maneuvers safely away from the iceberg.

And with that deft maneuver, you've rounded Cape Horn. Hooray!

Brandon runs below to check the radar to make sure there are no more icebergs in your path.

Oh, no! The radar screen is black. It's offline, and so is every other piece of navigational equipment on board. David goes below to try to figure out what's wrong.

Meanwhile, the iceberg you missed has forced you off course. You've drifted into the inlets that surround the rocky islands north of Cape Horn. Brandon uses a compass to help Jason steer around these dangerous islands. But the winds are extreme here. And the course is narrow. These gusts can drive the boat right into the rocks.

You return on deck and remain there with Georgina and Chelsea in case Brandon and Jason need you. Jason carefully steers to avoid the rocky shoreline and the other boats up ahead. The wind never stops. You hunch over to try to escape it—and you realize you look just like the trees that grow on these nearby islands. They grow bent over from the constant force of the wind.

These waters are grim—and are about to turn bleaker. In a few minutes a heavy fog rolls in—and you're sailing blind.

"I can't see a thing," Chelsea says, peering out into the heavy mist.

"There are islands and boats out there, but they're totally hidden," Georgina says. "It's sort of creepy."

You're all on the lookout, but you're afraid that by the time you can actually spot a rock or a boat in this dense fog, it will be too late. Should you continue sailing? You took Cape Horn because you thought it would be faster. You really don't want to stop now. But it might be safer to drop anchor in a cove and wait out the fog.

IF YOU DECIDE TO CONTINUE SAILING, TURN TO PAGE 181.

IF YOU DECIDE TO DROP ANCHOR, TURN TO PAGE 184.

Everyone sides with Georgina. You're relieved. You definitely didn't want Brandon's urine on your leg if it could be avoided!

The vinegar is poured on your skin. Georgina wears gloves to pry off the tentacles adhered to your leg, because even detached from the jellyfish, the tentacles can continue to sting. The acetic acid in the vinegar stops the stinging cells left on your leg from harming you, but Georgina must still call for a helicopter from Cairns, Australia, to whisk you away to the hospital. You will live, but your sea voyage is over. The only thing that hurts more than the box jellyfish sting right now is the sting of defeat.

THE END

Once the mainsail is tied with the reef knot, you're ready for the storm. It passes quickly, and the sun peeks out from the clouds. It's been a long time since you've felt its warmth on your face!

You're standing on deck with Georgina— and an albatross soars gracefully overhead. With its huge wingspan, it's one of the largest flying birds on earth. It glides on the same wind that sends your boat skipping across the ocean waves. Today you feel like you own the ocean. Today you remember why you love sailing.

You've been at sea for five months and three weeks— 175 days, to be exact—and you just rounded the Cape of Good Hope!

Georgina looks up at the soaring bird. "Some sailors think that seabirds carry the souls of dead sailors," she says. "That's why it's unlucky to kill them."

Before you can reply, the bottom of the boat hits a UFO!

At sea, that's an unidentified floating object. It's probably a lost shipping container or a lost oil barrel—but it found you.

IF YOU JUMP IN TO HELP CHELSEA, TURN TO PAGE 73.

IF YOU LET CHELSEA FIX THE RUDDER ALONE, TURN TO PAGE 45.

Life jackets will keep us afloat if something goes wrong with the raft is all that runs through your mind. Everything is moving really fast—and you should, too. You scoop up the bag of life jackets, rope, and flashlights and fall into the life raft alongside Jason.

And then that's it. It's over. The winds change direction as night gives way to dawn. The ocean becomes calm and the sun breaks through the clouds. Without your navigational equipment, you have only the vaguest idea where you are.

"Now what?" Chelsea demands.

"Just chill out and wait for rescue," Brandon replies.

Georgina gives Brandon a shove. "Move over. Your pointy elbow is jabbing my ribs."

"Well, you're totally leaning on me," you tell Georgina. "It's really tight in this thing."

The six of you are side by side in a tiny rubber life raft, without a centimeter of room between you.

"When will we be rescued?" Chelsea asks. Her voice is shrill. Anxiety clouds her usually determined eyes.

Everyone looks to David. "Never," he replies. "Nobody knows where we are."

"Don't think that way!" Jason scolds. "Of course we will. It will just take time."

"I'm hungry," Georgina complains.

"I can hear your stomach growling," Brandon taunts, nudging her shoulder out of his face.

Jason scans the life raft. It doesn't take long, since it's so small. "Where's the emergency grab bag?"

Everyone turns to you. "I—I—I just got the life jackets and flashlights," you stammer. "I could only grab one bag from the boat."

"Yum, I really want to eat a flashlight," Georgina replies sarcastically. She's becoming mean without food.

You realize now you made the wrong choice. The grab bag had food and other emergency supplies, including a handheld radio. "I'm sorry," is all you can say.

And then you all wait. And float. The sun beats down. All you want is a cool drink, but the grab bag has all your emergency water. The sun makes the ocean glitter around you. Cool glittery water. Everywhere.

"I'm so thirsty," Chelsea complains the next day through her cracked and bleeding lips.

"If we don't have fresh water, we'll die." Brandon says. His eyelids have swollen shut from sunburn.

"Just hold on," Jason implores. "Rescue will come."

But it doesn't. The hours warp together. Everyone is dizzy and faint. Reaching her hands over the side of the life raft, Chelsea scoops up the salt water.

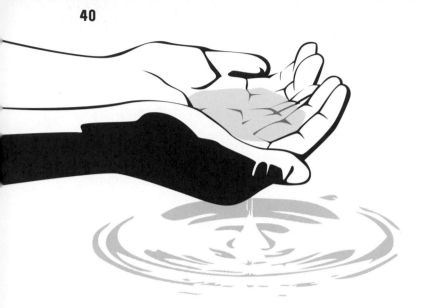

"Don't!" Jason cries in a brittle rasp.

She slurps the salty water anyway. Scoop. Slurp. You are too weak to pull her back. The more salt water she drinks, the thirstier she becomes. Then she begins to vomit uncontrollably. Her body shakes as she wretches. Dehydration eventually overwhelms Chelsea.

Rescue arrives a few hours later, but that's too late for poor Chelsea.

Months go by and Jason calls you at home. He wants to form another crew and try again. You refuse. The pain of losing Chelsea is too raw. Your sailing dreams have come to . . .

THE END

You kick off your deck shoes and dive in, clothes and all. The brown water is warm and murky. There is less than 10 feet between the yacht and the wall. You swim alongside the *Chronos II*, searching for the end of the line.

"Found it!" you cry. You lift it high, then begin to swim it toward the canal worker. A large cruise ship somewhere nearby blares its horn at the same moment the canal worker yells to you.

"What?" you call. Fragments of Spanish float back to you. You can't piece together what he's trying to say.

The lock gates click shut as you tread water, still trying to understand his warning.

After that, everything happens so fast. The chamber fills with the rush of thousands of gallons of water. You flail about helplessly, caught in the current, unsure whether to swim to the wall or back to the boat. Chelsea's high-pitched squeal calls your name.

The *Chronos II* has been nested, or tied, to a tugboat for the transit through the canal. Suddenly, the tugboat's stern swings away from the wall, violently pushing the *Chronos II* along with it. In less time than it takes to blink, the two boats are upon you. You are slammed full-force into the concrete lock wall. For minutes, you are pinned to the wall, the weight of the yacht crushing your ribs and blocking air from your lungs.

Pain ricochets through your body. You can hear your crewmates' screams of horror.

David blasts an emergency air horn to let everyone know you're in trouble. Jason and the tugboat skipper quickly redirect their boats away from you, but the damage is done. You leaped before you looked, and your dreams of glory have been crushed.

THE END

The Suez Canal will get you back to California three weeks faster and save thousands of miles sailing. Maybe you'll meet up with some pirates, but maybe you won't. It's worth the risk, everyone decides.

"Man the sails! We need to come about," Jason calls, setting sail for your new course.

Brandon grimaces, not pleased with the crew's choice. But over the next few days, it seems like a good one. The weather is hot and sunny with a steady breeze, and the *Chronos II* sails smoothly into the Gulf of Aden.

Brandon finds Jason at the wheel while you're scrubbing salt from the metal winches nearby. "Listen," Brandon says. "Sailing Pirate Alley is a big gamble. Since we're doing it, we have to stick to the IRTC."

"What's that?" you call.

"Internationally Recommended Transit Corridor," Brandon explains. "Along this 500-mile path, there are patrol ships that police the waterway. They bring the risk of a pirate attack way down. And that's important for a small yacht like ours, which is easy to board. Pirates have guns. They won't hesitate to use them."

The *Chronos II* sails alongside gigantic container ships, tankers, and car carriers on the IRTC over the next two days. Somalia, where most of the pirates are from, is a very poor African country with a weak government. The pirates know that if they hijack the ships in this area, the shipping companies will pay huge ransoms to get them back, and few pirates are ever punished.

The crew feels pretty safe while in the IRTC. You see several patrol boats. All is quiet. Then Jason and Brandon call the crew together. They are glaring at each other. Something is wrong.

"Tomorrow morning we leave the IRTC," Brandon announces. "We then have to make it through a hundred miles of pirate-infested waters unprotected." He shows the route on a chart

"What now?" Georgina asks.

"I think I should get on the radio and find other small boats in the area. We could cross together," Brandon suggests. "Pirates may be less likely to mess with a group."

"It could take days or even weeks to gather a flotilla," Jason counters. "Besides, a big group could attract unwanted attention. If we go it alone, we may be able to slip by unnoticed."

IF YOU WAIT FOR OTHER SHIPS, TURN TO PAGE 120.

IF YOU SAIL IT ALONE, TURN TO PAGE 139.

Chelsea has super-strong legs. She's a great swimmer—and you're not. The waters of the South Atlantic are the roughest you've met so far. The current is strong, the swells are huge, and the water is icy.

Chelsea lowers herself into the frigid ocean. Even with her drysuit—a special diving suit with a thermal undersuit to keep her warm—her lips turn blue. One thing's for sure—she can't stay in these waters too long.

In a few moments she resurfaces with the report that part of the rudder has broken off.

"When you scraped bottom in the Torres Strait, you must have weakened it," David says to you. "Whatever we just hit finished the job."

As David instructs Chelsea on the repair, the current pushes her. Then a wave hurls her away. She fights hard to swim back to try to replace the missing piece.

Then a huge wave barrels in.

Chelsea goes under.

Her head doesn't reappear for more than a minute.

Your pulse races as you search for some sign of her—a flash of her suit. A strand of hair. An air bubble.

Nothing.

"I'm jumping in," you say, when you can't wait any longer.

Jason and Brandon are ready to leap in, too.

And then she pops up.

"That was a big wave," she gasps.

You nearly collapse with relief.

⚓

The rudder is fixed and you sail on through the South Atlantic. The waves are enormous. The winds are out of control.

"Huge one coming!" David yells as another monster wave rushes the boat. Jason is at the wheel when the wave pounds the deck and knocks him off his feet, submerging him underwater.

When the water washes out. Jason is still holding the wheel, and he's already bracing himself for the next big one.

Everyone works hard to keep the boat upright. The wind and the waves toss it around as if it's a child's beach ball.

And this is a sunny day.

Georgina says a real storm is headed your way—and it's going to be a killer.

The storm hits early the next morning.

You hear a roar—and a gale-force wind slams the boat.

The boat flips on its side. You're thrown across the cabin and your back slams into the bulkhead. No, not the bulkhead. It's the deckhead—the ceiling.

"The keel is out of the water," Jason shouts, holding on to the table. "The mast is underwater."

Jason doesn't have to say anything more—this is danger of the worst kind.

"One strong wave will flip the boat totally and rip the mast from the deck," David says. "Snap it like a toothpick."

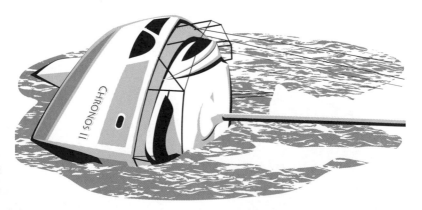

And everything would end. The challenge—and your lives.

Everyone grabs on to the nearest furniture.

No one can hide their fear. Not even Chelsea.

You can feel the boat struggling against the wild rocking sea. Struggling to right itself.

Then, with a crash, you're sitting on the floor again. The boat is upright.

You struggle to your feet and open the hatch to peek outside. The rain and the waves batter the deck. Even though it's morning, it's as dark as a grave out there. The wind whips the boat. You quickly close the hatch.

You wonder, *are we going to die?*

⚓

In a matter of hours, it's all over. The *Chronos II* has weathered through another storm.

"We made it!" you shout. You can't believe how lucky you are. Brandon is the only one with bad news. "We're way off course," he says.

"Then we have to make up the time," Jason says. "We have 98 days left to complete our trip. If we're lucky, we'll make it. But I don't like leaving things to luck."

"On this boat, that's risky," Georgina mutters.

"If we right ourselves and continue toward the Panama Canal, it could add two weeks to the schedule and we could blow the deadline," Jason says. "So instead we'll continue south and go around Cape Horn. It will be faster."

Faster—and more deadly.

Strong winds, huge waves, powerful currents, and treacherous icebergs—Cape Horn will give you the fight of your life.

Jules Jr. calls on the satellite phone to check on your progress. He votes for speed. "Take Cape Horn. You can do it!"

Jason and Chelsea agree.

Brandon, David, and Georgina vote for the Panama Canal.

It's up to you to break the tie among the crew.

IF YOU VOTE FOR CAPE HORN, TURN TO PAGE 87.

IF YOU VOTE FOR THE PANAMA CANAL, TURN TO PAGE 76.

"What are you waiting for?" Georgina demands, reaching for a line.

"Did you see that strange flash of light?" you ask, staring up. "I think it was a shooting star. If you wish on one, your wish will come true. I'm going to wish that our crew wins the million dollars."

"I'm wishing that you'd stop staring at the sky!" Georgina cries, as an enormous gust of wind suddenly fills the sails. The boat skids across the water, jolting you out of your stargazing daze. The wind picks up rapidly, going from 10 to 40 knots in only minutes. The mainsail pulls tight under the pressure, straining against the rigging.

"Pull the sail in now!" Georgina screams, as water rolls over the side and the boat tilts on its starboard edge.

Jason mans the wheel, trying desperately to even out the boat in the choppy seas. "All hands on deck!" he shouts. Then he turns to you. "Help Georgina shorten the sail! That's an order!"

You're embarrassed. It's not like you to be so flaky. You scramble to pull the sail in. The more area of the sail that is open to catch the wind, the more likely it is that a huge gust will push you over.

The sea turns dark and menacing. Rain pours down and seawater sweeps over you. Soaking wet and shivering, you try frantically to furl the jib and lower the mainsail, but there isn't enough time to get everything tied down properly. You wish you had started earlier.

A violent gust hits with incredible force, overpowering the boat and ballooning the sails. The line slips from your hand.

"Hold on!" Georgina shrieks. You grab the mast for dear life as a monster wave savagely crashes against the hull and the boat tilts and tilts. The sail smashes against the water, and the yacht capsizes.

Your heart sinks—and so do your million-dollar dreams.

THE END

You tie a bowline. David comes up just as you're tightening the loop. He scratches his head. "I know you're our rigging expert, but isn't that the wrong knot?"

"Of course it's not—" You stare at the knot and your cheeks flame pink. "Wow! I don't know what I was thinking. This knot forms a loop, like for throwing around a post."

It's so not like you to mess up a knot. You glance about. Everyone works frantically to keep the *Chronos II* upright. No one else has seen your mistake. "I'm sorry. Are you going to tell?" Jason and Mr. Houseman expect everyone to always bring their A-game.

"Our secret," David promises.

You quickly reef the mainsail using the correct reef knot. "Sail's secure!" you call to Chelsea. Jason steers the boat forward and the storm soon passes.

The *Chronos II* bounds through the Atlantic Ocean with a mild trade wind in the sails. Brandon checks and rechecks the weather reports, but there's no bad weather in sight.

A few days later that changes. Now Brandon is concerned. Super concerned. Out of nowhere, the tides become unpredictable. The current grows stronger as dusk falls. Soon, the sea rages.

Gale-force winds whip up mountainous waves. The *Chronos II* creaks and groans under the pressure. Then

everything starts to go wrong! The metal fittings break. A hole rips in the storm sail. The entire crew tries desperately to fix the problems. The winds make it feel as if a bulldozer is trying to flatten you.

Waves batter the port side, pushing the yacht farther and farther over on its heel. The *Chronos II* is nearly sideways! In moments, you will capsize.

"The life raft!" Brandon calls. "Everyone get in!"

"No!" David cries. "Stay on board."

IF YOU ABANDON SHIP, TURN TO PAGE 157.

IF YOU STAY ON THE BOAT, TURN TO PAGE 104.

It's called a grab bag for a reason, so you grab it. You know it's packed with emergency supplies—and this is definitely an emergency! You dive into the life raft just as the surging water sucks the *Chronos II* down to the ocean floor.

The six of you huddle in the cramped raft, bobbing on the vast ocean for hours. David can't get the emergency radio from the bag to work. "It's busted," he concludes.

"But someone is looking for us, right?" Chelsea asks.

"Houseman probably has a rough idea of where we were, but . . . we're not there anymore," Brandon says.

"So they may be looking in the wrong spot?" you clarify.

"Unfortunately, yes," David admits. "The current has been really strong since we've been floating. We've moved a long way from where the yacht went down."

"So what do we do?" Georgina demands.

"It's best to wait close to where we went down," Jason says. "Someone will find us eventually."

"Eventually?" Chelsea shrieks. "My skin is burned to a crisp, and we have only twenty energy bars to eat! There are two paddles. I say we start to row and try to find land."

IF YOU SIDE WITH CHELSEA, PICK UP A PADDLE AND ROW TO PAGE 82.

IF YOU SIDE WITH JASON, FLOAT ALONG TO PAGE 64.

Jason helps you raise a tarp-like canopy to shield the raft. The shade gives all of you some relief. Minutes tick by slowly, turning into hours.

"What's that?" Jason asks suddenly.

You hear it! The faint whir of a motor! Jason and David pull back the canopy. You scan the sea for a boat.

"Look up!" Georgina cries. "It's a plane!"

"We need to signal it!" David cries. He searches in the grab bag. "Where are the flares?"

For some strange reason, all the flares are missing.

"Now what?" Chelsea demands. "The plane will pass over us in less than a minute. This is our only chance."

"Our watches from Mr. Houseman are super shiny," Georgina says. "We can reflect the sun with them to signal the plane."

TO SIGNAL THE PLANE TURN TO PAGE 101.

"I think you should take the necklace off," you tell Chelsea.

Even though you'd rather snorkel alone, it's safer to swim in the ocean in a group.

"You two are such wimps," Chelsea says, laughing, but she agrees to leave the necklace behind.

In the water, you can't believe what you see—bright-red spiky urchins and a huge turtle that must weigh at least a hundred pounds.

Chelsea uses an underwater camera to snap photos of glowing fish that light up the sea with their eerie green color.

You check the fancy, expensive underwater watch Mr. Houseman gave each of you.

It's getting late.

It's not safe to be in the water at dusk. Fish get hungry at dusk, and you don't want to be their supper.

You should get out now.

You try to signal the girls, but they aren't paying any attention to you.

Stay calm, you tell yourself.

A parrot fish swims right by you. Its colors take your breath away, but that's not why your pulse starts to race and your heart begins to pound.

Up ahead, you see a fin. A shark fin.

And it's coming your way—fast.

SHARK!

THE TIGER SHARK CIRCLES . . .

"You did it!" You barely recognize your own voice. It comes out kind of squeaky.

Georgina and Chelsea scared the shark away. The fin grows fainter as it flees, but you can't tear your eyes from it.

You've drifted quite a distance from the yacht. Chelsea shouts out to the crew to come closer to pick you up.

You don't want to splash. Splashing might bring the shark back or attract another one nearby.

"Let's form a circle, with our backs toward the center," you say. "This way we'll be able to see out in three directions. Nothing will be able to sneak up on us."

The yacht slowly approaches.

You can barely breathe.

"Hurry up. Hurry up." You stare at the boat as it drifts slowly toward you.

"What's that?" Georgina suddenly yells.

"What?" Your whole body goes rigid with fear.

"Around Chelsea's neck," Georgina says. "She didn't take the necklace off."

"Give me a break," Chelsea says. "The two of you are wearing the watches Houseman gave us. They're shiny, too."

She has a point. You forgot about the watches.

But there's no time to argue—because the shark is back, and it looks angry.

"Don't splash," you warn the other two.

The shark swims in a wide circle around you. Your chest is tight. Your heart feels as if it's going to explode with fright.

The yacht nears.

The shark circles closer. Closer.

It gives you a long, hungry look—but then changes its mind and heads out to sea.

You quickly climb onto the boat.

You're the ones who were nearly shark food, but David is shaking. "Are you okay?" he asks.

"I've never been that close to a shark before. It was amazing!" Chelsea says.

David shakes his head. "Tiger sharks will eat anything. Even other sharks. You were very lucky."

David knows a lot about wildlife and is especially interested in endangered species—which is what you, Chelsea, and Georgina nearly became today!

⚓

Two days later, the gear for the steering mechanism arrives. David fixes it quickly, and you're off once again, sailing across the Pacific for Australia.

You are now on the longest stretch of your voyage without land. You'll be traveling more than 4,000 nautical miles alone at sea. That's at least one month, but more likely two, without seeing another boat. If something bad happens, there won't be anyone to help you. But on this cloudless day worry is not on the agenda.

Enjoy it while it lasts.

A week out from Hawaii, Jason orders you and David to do the daily boat inspection. You walk from bow to stern on both sides of the yacht, checking all the rigging. Then you check the hull, looking for cracks.

You report back to Jason. The boat is in good shape.

Georgina comes on deck and overhears. "That's good," she says. "Because a huge storm is headed our way. This one is real trouble."

"That can't be possible," you say. "Just look at the sky. It's perfect."

"For now," she says. "But not for long." She points north. "That's where it's coming from."

She can't be right. Weather predictions aren't always accurate, and you're sure she's way off target today.

You gaze out over the horizon, into the crystal-blue skies. Then, suddenly, ripples break the water.

You hear splashing—and a school of flying fish leap into the air. They glitter like jewels in the sunlight. Some land on the deck.

You were starting to feel very isolated out here in the mighty Pacific. The flying fish show up just in time. Now you don't feel quite so alone.

Later that night, the sea turns calm. Too calm. The stillness is creepy. The boat inches forward. You and Brandon gaze at the stars overhead.

"No wind tonight," Jason says as he heads below. "You can man the helm, Brandon."

"Gee, thanks," Brandon says.

A strange flash in the sky catches your eye, but before you can get a good look Georgina appears.

"Take down the sails," she says. "Right now. The storm is coming."

IF YOU HURRY TO TAKE DOWN THE SAILS, TURN TO PAGE 106.

IF YOU TRY TO LOCATE THE STRANGE FLASH IN THE SKY, TURN TO PAGE 51.

"The only thing rowing to nowhere will do is exhaust us," you say. "Until we see land or another boat or something to head toward, we should stay put and conserve our energy."

Everyone agrees. You sit back and wait for rescue.

And wait.

And wait.

Your stomach growls with hunger. Hours pass without the sight of anything but ocean. You play Twenty Questions and Truth or Dare. You hear about everyone's families and pets. You learn their favorite colors, favorite animals, and favorite foods.

"Enough with the food talk. I'm starving," Chelsea says.

"I've got to eat something," Brandon chimes in. "Now."

Everyone agrees. You crawl over Georgina and open the grab bag. "We have twenty protein bars, two cans of turnips, two cans of green beans, and two cans of peaches." You scrounge around. "A package of raisins, a package of hard candies."

"Plus the thirty foil packets of fresh water," Jason adds.

"I call the peaches!" Brandon yells.

"You can't call food," you tell him. "We need to share."

"And ration," Chelsea adds, swatting Brandon's hand away from the can. "No one is looking in the right place for us. We could be floating out here for months!"

Everyone chooses you to ration the food. You assess the situation. "The protein bars have a lot of calories. The hard candies will help our parched throats."

"Hand me a water packet," Brandon says. "My lips are cracking in the sun."

You find a small cup in the bag and pour out a tiny bit. "A person can survive for weeks without food but will die in days without fresh water." You divide the cans of green beans among the six of you. Brandon's not satisfied. He wants more. When you refuse him, he glares at you.

"Our best bet is to sleep or rest," Georgina advises, when David vomits over the side of the bobbing raft. "It will help the seasickness."

For the next three days, you ration the food. The protein bars taste gross, like dense, dry coconut cookies. Nevertheless, you salivate at the sight of them. The pain of hunger in your stomach turns into a pit of fear. You haven't told anyone, but you are down to only three bars, the two cans of peaches, and three bags of water. With six of you, that won't last two more days.

You finally fall asleep with your arms around the bag . . . and wake to the unmistakable sound of crinkling foil. Brandon is unwrapping a protein bar! You gasp when you spot the two cans of peaches by his feet. Each one is open and empty!

"I'm—I'm sorry," Brandon stammers. "I was just so hungry—"

"And you don't think the rest of us are hungry, too?" Chelsea screams.

Brandon buries his face in his hands. His body shakes with sobs. He is totally losing it.

You can't believe Brandon pried the bag from your arms, but yelling at him won't bring back the food. You all need every ounce of energy just to survive.

The rest of the day is spent in silence. The brutal rays of the sun beat down, scorching your already painful sunburns. Now you fear, especially with your limited food supply, that the heat will speed up dehydration.

TURN TO PAGE 56.

You're going after the watch. It's way too special to let it end up in some huge fish's stomach. But then the faint cry of voices catches your attention. Voices calling your name. Voices from your crewmates. They're waving at you. Waving you toward the boat. Out of the corner of your eye, you can see the watch's shiny face shimmer in the sunlight. It's drifting farther and farther away.

It's now or never, so you turn your back on the crew and swim after the watch.

The flippers on your feet give you speed and make your kicks more powerful. In order to swim faster, you push the snorkel mask on top of your head, letting the tube dangle alongside your mouth. Kicking rapidly and keeping your head raised so the watch's glint stays in sight, you splash through the water. Your lungs suck in air as you fight against the current. Your muscles ache, but you won't give up.

You're getting that watch.

But no matter how fast you swim, the waves push the watch just out of reach. Kicking with all your strength sends sprays of salt water into the air. Only a few more strokes and you're there.

Your hand clutches the watch and holds it tight. Your breath comes out in sharp rasps as you tread water and slip it back on your wrist, impressed it's still ticking.

What time is it? you wonder. But after brushing the water out of your eyes to check, something besides the second hand catches your eye. Something slicing through the water. Something deadly.

It's a shark fin. Then another . . . and another. Looks like your shark is back, and this time he brought friends. It's three against one—you're outnumbered in this deadly match.

Your body stiffens, and you wrap your arms around yourself in a frightened hug. Your watch ticks away the seconds before the attack. Now you remember something else you learned during *Shark Week*. Sharks are attracted to shiny objects.

Your time is up!

THE END

If you try to swim over the waves, they will fling your body like a Frisbee in a tornado. You know your only hope is to swim under them. You keep your eyes on the foamy white crests in the water. The next wave forms, growing larger and larger as it picks up speed. The lip of water curls menacingly, threatening to suck you in.

Just as the wave is about to overtake you, you fill your lungs with air, then dive down, plunging deep under the roiling surf. You aim your body toward the bottom.

Everything is calm and peaceful under the rolling waves. You glide forward and frog-kick gently. The ocean gives little resistance this deep. Fish swim alongside you, accepting you as one of their own. But as your lungs begin to burn, you know you aren't a fish. Air. You need air! You must get to the surface. Now!

Kicking with all your might, you propel yourself upward. You break through the water and inhale the wonderful, fresh air. Then you notice the waves. They're gone. The ocean is now calm. You pivot about, amazed at how far you swam.

Oh, no. Where is the *Chronos II*?

You turn in circles, squinting at the horizon. Searching, searching. *This can't be right,* you think. Your heart pounds in your ears as the realization hits you—they must be looking for you in the other direction. Or they think you've drowned.

You are all alone.

Wait! There is something in the distance. You swim closer to get a better view. No, it's not the *Chronos II*. It's just a tiny speck of land with a solitary palm tree.

You hope the tree has some coconuts, because this little island is yours for now. Sure, you'll eventually be rescued, but until then, welcome home.

THE END

As soon as you announce you're staying and offer your fix-it expertise, Brandon breaks free of Georgina's iron grip. "I'll help, too—"

David cuts him off. "Brandon, there's no room in the small space for anyone else. Really. Chelsea, you go, too."

"Exactly," Jason agrees. "Both of you go on deck with Georgina and disengage the lifeboat. Get everything ready in case this doesn't work." He stares at the now knee-deep water. "Grab life jackets."

Chelsea hesitates but then follows Jason's orders. "Work fast," she warns as she leaves with Brandon.

You, David, and Jason squeeze into the saloon. David points out the crack to the right of the table. David taps the fiberglass hull near the crack with the handle of a screwdriver. Despite the pounding waves, you can hear a hollow sound.

"Oh, boy," David mutters. "It would've been a lot better if that sounded solid. We've got major damage. Our only hope is to patch it with epoxy until someone can rescue us," David says.

"Will it hold?" Jason demands. The waves continue to pummel the *Chronos II*.

"I don't know," David admits. He smears the thick, gray epoxy on the crack.

The water creeps up your legs, toward your hips.

David groans. Not a good sign.

"The epoxy won't hold!" you cry. "Everything is too wet."

Another big wave batters the hull and the crack widens before your eyes. Water rushes in. In seconds, it is up to your armpits.

"We need to get out!" Jason orders. But David won't quit. He keeps trying to repair the crack, even after it becomes a gaping hole and the sea rushes into the boat.

Water covers your neck, your face, your head. There's no air. You search for a way out. But you've waited too long.

This is . . .

THE END

It's too dangerous to let Chelsea fix the rudder alone, you convince everyone. You are going to help her.

Chelsea dives in first to check out the bottom of the boat. "Whatever we hit snapped the rudder." Her voice quivers from the icy-cold water when she resurfaces.

David says it can be fixed, and he has the perfect piece of wood to make the repair.

"Be careful with this," he says as he hands it to you. "This is the only piece on board that will do the job."

You dive into the water with the wood, and you are nearly paralyzed by the cold. The frigid current catapults you away from the boat. Chelsea is struggling too, but she has superstrong legs. She's winning the battle. You're not.

"Give it to me!" Chelsea reaches out for the wood as you fight your way back to her.

You stretch your arm out to hand it to her, but the monster current is too strong. It rips the wood from your grip.

"Oh, no!" Chelsea's eyes grow wide with disbelief as you both watch the wood ride the wild waves, taking your dream of winning with it.

THE END

Jason will have to maneuver the boat back on course so you can sail through the Panama Canal. It won't be easy. You'll be sailing against the wind.

It's late at night. You listen to the shriek of the gale-force winds as you head to your berth. The boat pitches like crazy—and you're hurled across the cabin.

Your head crashes into Jason's berth on the opposite side.

"We should have gone around Cape Horn," you say to Brandon. "It couldn't be much worse than this. And it would have been faster."

Brandon laughs. "If we took Cape Horn, we'd have to sail through the Roaring Forties and the Furious Fifties! Sailing the latitudes between 40 and 59 degrees is much worse than this. The wind speeds there are wild. The waves are at least 20 feet high. In the Furious Fifties you can hit a rogue wave 100 feet high! Trust me. This is much better."

A wall of water crashes over the deck. The wind whips the boat in the churning sea. Time is running out.

If you blow the schedule and lose this race, it will be *your* fault. But only a submarine can survive in this ocean, you think. How much more of this punishment can the *Chronos II* take?

⚓

But miraculously, you make it through another storm.

"Am I good or what!" Jason says.

You have to agree. He brought the boat through the mid-Atlantic faster than anyone thought possible. Now you're sailing along the coast of South America, only about a week away from the Panama Canal.

You have forty-five days to make it back in time to win the money.

Brandon and Georgina study the charts and the weather. They think you'll be able to do it in forty days.

It will be tight, but today no one is thinking about that.

Today there's a steady breeze. The weather is calm. And you're all relaxing.

To have fun, Chelsea climbs the mast.

"Come down now," David tells her. "That's high enough."

But Chelsea just laughs.

"Be right back," you tell Brandon. "I'm going to get my fishing rod."

You've been fishing all week with Brandon, and you haven't caught a single fish. Maybe today is your day.

You go below to get your gear.

As you head back through the cabin, your eye catches a flash of purple on Georgina's bunk. You take a closer look. It's a diary. You know you shouldn't read it, but if you do, maybe it will give you a clue—maybe you'll find out why she acts so strangely.

You pick it up—but you hear footsteps. You quickly drop it, and pass her on the steps.

⚓

"I'd love to catch a blue marlin one day," Brandon says.

The blue marlin is one of the largest fish on Earth. It can measure up to 13 feet long and weigh close to 2,000 pounds.

"I'd be happy with a snapper or a tuna," you say.

No sooner than you say "tuna," Brandon hooks one, but it gets away.

You fish some more. You reel in nothing—and then . . .

"Did you see that?" you ask Brandon. "I think I have something on the line."

Your rod quivers. Something is biting. You snap back your rod and start reeling in.

You can't wait to see what you caught. Your rod bends harder. You pull back and keep reeling. The fish puts up a fight. But you're winning the battle. Finally, it appears on the surface. You swing it on deck.

"What is *that*?" you say.

Brandon shakes his head. "I don't know," he says. "Never saw anything like *that* before."

It has red stripes with spines sticking up from its back.

Even though you don't know what it is, you want to keep it. You'd love to cook it and make a surprise dinner for the crew tonight.

IF YOU COOK THE FISH FOR THE CREW, TURN TO PAGE 186.

IF YOU DECIDE TO THROW IT BACK, TURN TO PAGE 126.

"Catch you later!" you call to Chelsea and Georgina, as you cannonball off the side. Since you set sail, you haven't had a minute alone. *Snorkeling by myself is going to be great*, you think, and you won't have to see anyone until dinnertime.

The ocean is quiet. You cut across the gentle waves with sure, strong strokes. The rhythmic splash of your kicks sets a steady pace. Farther and farther from the boat you swim.

You flip over and float on your back, staring at the puffy clouds in the brilliant blue sky. Your body feels weightless in the warm water, and you let the tide move you along. Squinting against the glare of the sun, you decide the far left cloud looks like Idaho and the one in the center looks like an ice-cream cone. The one to the right . . . you almost laugh out loud. That cloud looks like a sailboat! You have to show the crew.

You turn back to wave to them—and you are in for your first shock: the yacht is a tiny dot in the distance.

And the second shock is headed your way.

It's a shark—and it's aiming right for you!

The shark slices through the water like a bullet. Its sharp, powerful teeth glint in the sun. Your heart pounds, and you find it hard to breathe. You have to remind yourself to tread water and stay calm.

Suddenly, it's only inches away! *Move!* your brain screams. Panicked, you jerk to the right just in time, and the

shark narrowly misses you. It bumps your hip, scraping you with its thick, sandpaper-like skin. You are bleeding, and the fresh wound burns in the salt water.

Your eyes widen as the shark turns and sets its sights—and jaws—on you once again.

Do something, you tell yourself, *before it's too late!*

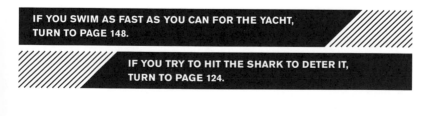

IF YOU SWIM AS FAST AS YOU CAN FOR THE YACHT, TURN TO PAGE 148.

IF YOU TRY TO HIT THE SHARK TO DETER IT, TURN TO PAGE 124.

You're all too restless to just sit. Everyone votes to paddle except Jason. Jason realizes he has been outvoted, so he grabs one paddle. You take the other.

There's very little room to paddle. You are all squeezed together like Junior Mints melted at the bottom of the candy box. For a moment, you close your eyes and imagine you are in an air-conditioned movie theater back home.

"Which way are we heading?" Chelsea asks.

Back to reality. You open your eyes, squinting in the glare of the sun. To the left lies an endless expanse of water. To the right, the same. Everyone surveys the lonely stretch of the Southern Atlantic Ocean.

"Go that way." David points toward the left.

"Why?" Chelsea asks.

"I'm a lefty," David explains sheepishly.

No one has a better idea, so you head left.

"One! Two! We should row in sync," Jason instructs.

You move your arms to the rhythm. "One! Two!" The crew takes up the chant. The raw, sunburned skin on your arms and neck stretches painfully with every movement.

"One! Two!" You and Jason paddle for what feels like hours. Every muscle cries out in pain, and sweat drips off your forehead and into your eyes. The air is hot and heavy.

When you can row no longer, you switch out with Brandon, open a can of turnips and share them with Jason and David. You have to ration what little food you have.

"Turnips?" Jason gags. "Gross, David! Why'd you pack those?"

"I like turnips," David retorts.

You don't. You peer into the grab bag: just canned vegetables and protein bars. Little do you realize how badly you will crave turnips when you are down to just one bar. For the next four days, the raft is in constant motion. Everyone takes turns rowing. It's hard to make any headway with the small paddles.

As the hours pass in the sun with very little food and only sips of fresh water, you grow dizzy from the heat and exertion. You're rowing again, and your shoulders throb. Every movement makes you weaker than weaker.

"One . . . two . . ." Jason mumbles feebly.

Oh, please. You gave up synchronized counting long ago.

You drift aimlessly. In all this time, you haven't seen land. You've just paddled around and around in circles. Getting nowhere. Going nowhere. And no one has found you.

But you won't give up. You'll keep rowing until your body gives out in . . .

THE END

It's better to risk bad weather than risk your lives, you all finally decide.

The Indian Ocean finally starts behaving as expected. The winds pick up and the waves grow huge. These days you're either cold and wet or tired and wet or hungry and wet. It rains and rains. The gray seeps into your bones. You've never been on a boat this long. You're lonely for home.

Jason has a black canvas bag on deck that holds a couple of heavy rain jackets, much better than yours. He takes one and gives you one, then tosses the bag aside.

Georgia comes around to inspect the sails for any tears. Her gaze rests on Jason's bag. Then, before you can say a word, she picks up the bag and throws it over the side.

You can't believe what you've just seen. But you don't say anything. You don't want a fight to break out, and you hope Jason thinks his bag flew overboard. Georgina is dependable and responsible. But she's also a little crazy, and you wonder if you'll ever find out why.

⚓

"Come quick!" David yells a couple of weeks later. He sounds frantic, which is very unlike him.

As you climb the steps, something rams the boat. You're slammed against the bulkhead. Everyone else is already on deck.

BAM! The boat is hit again.

You pull yourself to the top step. Clutched by fear, you look around quickly for the ship that hit you. But there's nothing there, just miles and miles of empty gray sea.

The crew stands at the bow of the boat, gazing down into the water. That's when you see the huge, dark shadow.

A whale.

You've never seen one this close before. It's twice as long as your yacht.

With a blast of spray from its blowhole, it leaps out of the water. If it lands on the boat, it will crush you instantly.

The whale crashes next to you with a huge splash and rocks the boat madly.

86

Everyone goes sprawling across the deck. David's head hits the floor with a sickening thud.

The crew let down their guard in the calm water—no one is wearing a safety harness. Another leap like that, and you'll all drown.

You watch in horror as the whale soars up again. It crashes down, closer this time. Chelsea slides across the deck. Jason reaches for her arm and yanks her back.

The whale disappears under the boat—then swims away.

David rubs his head. "That was a pygmy blue whale. The smaller type of blue whale."

"If that's the small one, I hope we never meet the big one," you say.

⚓

A few hours later, a nasty storm rolls in. Chelsea, still a little wobbly from the whale incident, asks you to help lash the mainsail to the boom.

What kind of knot do you use?

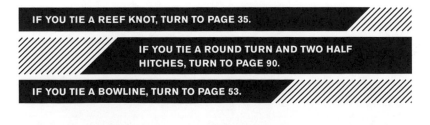

IF YOU TIE A REEF KNOT, TURN TO PAGE 35.

IF YOU TIE A ROUND TURN AND TWO HALF HITCHES, TURN TO PAGE 90.

IF YOU TIE A BOWLINE, TURN TO PAGE 53.

"Take Cape Horn. You can do it!" Mr. Houseman's words ring in your ear. You don't want to disappoint him.

"Cape Horn!" you vote.

The color drains from David's face. Georgina and Brandon shake their heads in disbelief.

"Big mistake," Brandon mutters. "Really big mistake."

"Why?" Your voice comes out in a croak.

"Let's put it this way—there's a statue on Cape Horn of an albatross. It was built in memory of the hundreds of sailors who drowned trying to round the cape."

"Maybe we should rethink this," you say to Jason and Chelsea.

"He's just trying to scare you," Chelsea says. "Besides, we voted. The decision is made."

"Let's stop wasting time talking about it," Jason says. "We're going to sail around Cape Horn. It's the ultimate challenge! We're going to earn our gold rings!"

"Gold rings? What does that mean?" David asks.

"In the 1700s and 1800s, sailing around Cape Horn was a popular trade route for sailors carrying goods from Australia to Europe. If they made it around the Horn, each sailor earned the right to wear a gold hoop earring in his left ear—the ear that faced the Horn as they sailed around it," Jason explains.

You want to take back your vote and head for the Panama Canal, but it doesn't matter what you want because Jason has his mind made up. You're sailing around Cape Horn.

"Time to earn our gold earrings," you say.

Brandon shakes his head in disgust. "Or die trying."

⚓

Jason and Brandon chart your new course around the tip of South America—Cape Horn. This part of the world has the most treacherous seas on Earth. You're sailing through the latitude range called the Furious Fifties, and now you know why they got that name. The powerful winds blow constantly here. They pound the boat with punishing gusts. The waves are enormous and the currents are lethal. These forces are so strong, they take your breath away.

The sailors' graveyard. That's what Cape Horn is called, and those words haunt you as the *Chronos II* battles the raging sea.

We'll never survive this, you think, but there's no time for regrets, because a squall suddenly turns up and hits the boat without warning. It hammers the yacht with 60-mile-per-hour winds. You grip the rail as the boat twists and turns and corkscrews, fighting to stay upright.

Brandon, Chelsea, and Georgina wrestle with the sails. The rain and hail sting their skin as they secure the rigging.

Brandon runs from Chelsea to Georgina, trying to help them both at the same time. David charges downstairs to make sure everything is tied down tight.

"No visibility!" Jason shouts to you and Brandon from the wheel. "Help me navigate! Check the radar!"

"I can't leave what I'm doing," Brandon yells.

"I'll go!" You race downstairs.

You dodge Brandon's lunch plate as it soars through the cabin like a Frisbee. David is on the floor, picking up papers.

You leap over him and reach the navigation table and the radar. There's a green dot on the screen. You and David don't know what it is.

Should you take Brandon away from his post to take a look at it? Or just wait and see if it goes away?

IF YOU DECIDE TO GET BRANDON, TURN TO PAGE 31.

IF YOU DECIDE TO WAIT, TURN TO PAGE 74.

You quickly tie a round turn and two half hitches. Your fingers move automatically without your brain focusing. You're too busy watching Georgina. What is she doing? She stands nose-to-nose with the mast in the rain. "Where is it? Where is it?" she cries.

You hurry to her side. "What's wrong with the mast?"

"The silver coin I attached to it before we left is gone." Georgina's eyes are filled with anxiety. "We need to find it!"

You see it glint on the deck. "There," you point.

Georgina dives for the coin. "Why did you attach a coin to the mast?" you ask, but Georgina doesn't hear you in the powerful wind. The next huge gust rips across the deck, strains the sail, and pulls the lines taut. The knot you just tied, attaching the mainsail to the boom, loosens. Oh, no! You tied the wrong knot. You should have tied a reef knot.

The sail flaps furiously. Other lines along the mast begin to break loose. The sail is now secured only at the mast. The boat heels dangerously.

"I can't steer without the sail!" Jason screams. "Someone do something!"

"I'm on it!" Chelsea cries over the wind. She hoists herself onto the mast.

Chelsea uses her strong arms to pull herself up, up, up.

"She shouldn't be up there," Georgina warns.

Your stomach twists with guilt. She's up there because you tied the wrong knot.

Chelsea sways with the mast in the violent winds. The sail and loose line whip across the boat, just out of her reach.

Jason tries desperately to control the rocking boat. "Drop anchor!" he calls to you. "Hurry!"

You race to the bow where the anchor is stored. As you crouch to pull it out, you hear a high-pitched scream and whirl around to see Chelsea free-falling through the air.

THUD! Her body smashes onto the deck.

Everyone rushes over. Chelsea doesn't move. Her leg is twisted at a strange angle. Georgina puts her ear to Chelsea's mouth. "She's still breathing. David, we need medical help out here. Radio for a boat, a helicopter, something. Fast!"

Everyone springs into action. Within an hour Georgina has her stabilized, but it takes another day for help to arrive. As she is hoisted into the rescue helicopter, you are all relieved to see her getting the medical help she needs. But with no more sailing for Chelsea, for your crew, it's . . .

THE END

Rami leaves. Boats come and go. But the *Chronos II* must wait until Mr. Houseman sorts everything out. Sand blows in from the Sinai desert, coating everything in a layer of grime. Your days are spent cleaning every nook, winch, and cranny.

One night, Rami's boat reappears. "Sick of waiting?" he calls. "Ready to make a deal now?"

"Never!" you all shout.

"You'll be sorry," Rami threatens, before he motors off.

"What does he mean?" Georgina asks nervously.

"Oh, please!" Brandon scoffs. "He can't bully us."

David runs onto the deck. "I just heard from Mr. Houseman. We're finally cleared. He got us a pilot for tomorrow morning."

"Excellent!" Georgina lets out a sigh of relief.

You're itching to get through the canal and into the open ocean to make up the wasted time. You take first watch while everyone sleeps. Hundreds of stars twinkle overhead. You see Ursa Major, the constellation in the shape of a bear, and the bright North Star. You marvel how ancient sailors used the stars to navigate. No computers, no GPS.

Then you notice a light in the darkness. The light moves closer. The light is on a motorboat.

A motorboat filled with men.

RAMI'S MEN FORCE YOUR CREW INTO THE LIFE RAFT, BEFORE THEY STEAL YOUR BOAT.

GET IN! NOW!

GRAB SUPPLIES!

FLOAT ON TO PAGE 38.

You race toward the bow, slipping and sliding. The mast looms overhead, then hits the stern deck with an ominous BOOM, completely missing you.

You and Chelsea are safe—for now.

But without a mast to hold the sails up, they drop in a heap. Your heart sinks as you watch them drag in the ocean. Chelsea stares wide-eyed and begins to shake. The *Chronos II* jerks about unsteadily. It lurches from side to side, bouncing you and Chelsea about like the little silver balls in a pinball machine. Desperately, you try to grab onto something to steady yourself.

You need to clip your safety harness onto the lifeline. You should have done it long ago. Now everything is too slippery and the boat is rocking rapidly. It's impossible to maintain your balance long enough to clip on.

"Jason! David! Help!" you cry. You've spotted your crewmates' heads peering out from the hatch. They don't hear you. They stare in shock at the damage to the mast and the stern. Will they be able to save the sails and repair the boat? They don't have much time before vital pieces are swept out to sea.

No one sees you and Chelsea fighting for your lives by the bow.

"Hold on, Chelsea!" you scream as the two of you cling, white-knuckled, to a mooring cleat. The stern of the boat sinks in the storm. The bow raises in the air, pulling you down, weakening your faltering grip.

Then a wave breaks on the hull. It rips your hands from the cleat and catapults you into the sea! The shock of the cold water sends a searing pain jolting throughout your body. You try to scream, but no sound comes out.

Luckily, Chelsea screams loud enough for both of you. For a tiny girl, she has amazing lung power!

Jason, David, Georgina, and Brandon hook up their safety harnesses and race to the edge.

"Brandon, get the big flashlight! David, throw a line—fast!" Jason barks. "Keep your heads up!" he bellows to you.

"Hurry!" Georgina screams. "They're going to drown!"

David flings a life ring, and you grab hold. Your teeth chatter loudly as David and Brandon work together to pull you onto the boat. Georgina and Jason have already rescued Chelsea.

"We lost our chance," Jason mutters once you're back on board. Bits of sail and mast now drift far out to sea. If you'd been harnessed, the crew wouldn't have had to spend precious time rescuing you and could have saved the sail and mast. Maybe then David could've patched things together.

Now you will need to radio for a tow. Your adventure is all washed up.

THE END

You're afraid that the canopy will trap the heat as if you were closed up in a car's trunk on a summer day. The crew decides to keep it folded away.

The life raft floats. The sun beats down. You close your eyes. The thick heat claws at your body, and your lips blister painfully. By noon, the sun is high in the sky, and your world has begun to spin. Up is no longer up and down is no longer down. Your brain is so foggy, so confused.

Opening one eye, you squint at your crewmates. They have all been hit hard by the sun. Everyone's skin is pink and raw. Everyone's eyes look dry and sunken. Rummaging about in the supply bag for fresh water, you rip open one of the foil packets and suck down the liquid. Then you reach for another.

"Stop!" David cries. "We need to save it for later."

"But I'm so thirsty," you protest. "My mouth feels like it is filled with cotton."

"We're all thirsty," David says, and there's no arguing with that. You're desperate, though. Dehydration is making you nauseated and irritable.

"I need it!" you cry and grab another water packet before anyone can stop you. You greedily guzzle it down. Ripping open another, you chug that one, too. And then you begin to vomit uncontrollably.

"Gross!" Chelsea shrieks as your barf splatters onto her.

"You drank too fast," Georgina explains. "If you don't stop throwing up, you'll dehydrate even more."

How can you stop? You feel so sick. So out of it.

You try to speak but can't get the words out. Your lips and tongue are swollen. There is no moisture anywhere in your body. You are no longer sweating in the heat. Flipping over on your stomach, you lower your face closer, closer, closer to the cool water. A long silver fish swims up to you. He opens his mouth and smiles.

"Oh, my God!" you cry. "The fish has braces!"

Georgina tells everyone you are having delusions from dehydration.

No way! This fish has definitely been to the orthodontist! If you can just submerge your face, you can see it better . . .

SPLASH! You tumble into the ocean and spiral downward. The sun has zapped your strength. You couldn't take the heat, so this is . . .

THE END

All six of you aim the silver mirrored watch faces simultaneously at the sun.

"Pilots have reported seeing flashes from miles away if the weather is clear and you get the right angle," David reports. Luckily, there's not a cloud in the clear, blue sky. The brilliant rays of the sun reflect off the shiny surfaces and bounce into the path of the passing plane.

You hold your breath and tighten your grip on your watch. Did the plane see you? Did it notice the strange beams of light?

You tilt your watch up and down, aiming the reflected sunlight again and again.

The plane flies overhead. It keeps flying and flying until it is a dot in the distance and then completely out of sight. The gentle slapping of the waves fills the void of the whirring engine.

"You can put your watch down," Georgina says gently. "It's gone."

"No! No! The plane can't be gone!" You sound hysterical, but you can't help it. Your chance of rescue just flew away. Burying your head in your hands, you will yourself not to cry.

"I hear—" Jason starts.

"Me too," David says.

"It circled back!" Chelsea screams. Everyone raises their eyes to the sky, and sure enough, the plane has returned. You cheer and whistle and wave your watches. The plane circles four more times. Each time it descends lower.

"They see us!" Brandon cries. "I know they do!"

"Look! They're throwing something out of the plane," Georgina says.

A bright-orange marker buoy hits the water and bobs alongside the raft. Then the plane flies off. "What the—!" Chelsea throws up her arms in outrage.

"Don't worry," David says. "They're coming back for us."

It's almost dark when the first rescue helicopter appears, zeroed in by the marker buoy. Then another arrives. Helicopters can fly lower than planes, so that's why they've been sent to rescue you.

Rescue is tricky, but soon all six of you are plucked from the raft and hoisted into the waiting helicopters. They fly you to Cape Town, South Africa, where you are all treated for dehydration and heatstroke before flying on Mr. Houseman's private plane back to California.

You're back to where you started, but this wasn't how you were supposed to get here.

There are no cheering crowds. There are no TV cameras filming your successful return.

"This stinks," Jason mutters.

"We could do it again," you suggest. "All of us. We'll start from the beginning, but this time we'll make better choices." You turn to your crewmates. "Are you all in?"

IF YOU'RE ALL IN, TURN BACK TO PAGE 13.

You stay on the boat. The *Chronos II* is upright—well, barely, but it's always smarter to stay aboard than risk the open water in a tiny lifeboat.

Waves explode onto the port side one after another. BAM! BAM! BAM! There's no time to recover before the next one hits. The deck is ankle-deep in seawater. Everyone hurries below for safety. The sails are furled. There's no thought of steering or sailing. The only concern is survival.

David straps himself into his berth. "Hold on tight!" he yells over the terrifying roar of the water.

"What a great roller coaster!" Brandon tries to joke, but no one laughs.

"I was on a boat during Hurricane Earl, but this storm is worse than that," Chelsea confides.

BAM! The crash of water against the hull is deafening.

"Those sound like the largest waves I've ever heard." Jason's eyes are wide.

You huddle on the floor beneath your berth, numb with fear and soaked with seawater. You're so wet you don't notice it at first. But soon it's impossible to miss. "We have a leak!"

What starts as a trickle rapidly turns to a gush, and the water spreads across the floor. David and Jason scramble to investigate. Water collects under the berths on the port side.

Brandon tries to grab his stray socks
and underwear, now floating
along the floor.

"The hull cracked!" Jason
calls. "Even worse, it's below
the waterline," he cries.

"We have to get out
of here," Georgina says.
"Or we'll drown."

"Wait!" David calls.
"I think I can patch it. I
just need one or two of
you to help."

"I'll help," Chelsea offers.
"The rest of you should go to the life raft."

"I'm staying," Jason announces. "A captain
never abandons his boat with people still on it."

"Brandon and I will get the life raft ready." Georgina's
already tugging Brandon up the stairs.

What will you do?

IF YOU HELP DAVID, TURN TO PAGE 71.

IF YOU HEAD FOR THE LIFE RAFT, TURN TO PAGE 29.

You really want to search the sky for another flash of light. So far everyone on board has seen a shooting star except you. This could be your night.

But you jump up and start to take the sails down just in case Georgina is right after all. You know sometimes there's a calm before a storm.

As you work, the wind suddenly picks up.

WHAM! A gust strikes the mainsail with such force, the mast quakes. You're sure the mast is coming down.

The wind is blowing at least 50 knots. On land, that would bring down trees. Your pulse races as the waves crest high above the yacht. *Where is Jason?* you wonder. *How can he sleep through this?*

Brandon helps you with the sails, then goes below to clean up. Everything he owns is scattered in the galley, in his berth, and on the chart table. In this kind of weather, his stuff could go flying and hit someone with the force of a bullet.

The wind dies down a bit, then picks up—and a monster wave forms. The stern rises as the yacht is caught in its curl.

You hold your breath and cling to the lifeline as the yacht tilts more and more—then the black sky is split by a swift bolt of lightning.

You shriek as it nearly strikes the mast. The sky opens up and the rain pelts down.

Chelsea appears on deck, yelling something over the crashing waves.

Another bolt of white lightning illuminates the sky and reveals her face. You're surprised at what you see.

There's no fear in her eyes. She's excited—and that can be dangerous in a storm like this. Sometimes a little fear can save a life. You don't want to leave Chelsea up here alone. She might do something reckless.

Down below, you can't believe what you see—Brandon is hiding under the dining table. Georgina is gripping the chart table with one hand, trying to strap down the laptop with the other.

Before you can say anything, a shoe comes soaring at you. It's a big shoe—Brandon's. "Ow!" you cry out as it clips you in the shoulder.

Brandon's head pops up from the table. "Great! You found it!" he says, holding the other one up.

You look aft and see David and Jason on the floor in front of Jason's berth.

"I need your help," David shouts. "Jason fell out of his berth. He's bleeding."

"Jason was taking a nap," David explains. "He didn't have the lee cloth attached." That's the canvas material that attaches to the open side of the bunk so the sleeper doesn't fall out during rough seas.

"When the boat pitched, Jason rolled out and Brandon's book flew off his bed. It gashed Jason's eye. "

David shakes his head in disgust. "I keep telling Brandon to put his stuff away. He never listens."

You quickly open the storage compartment next to Jason's berth and find the first-aid kit. As you pull the kit down from the shelf, the yacht pitches heavily. The first-aid kit flies from your hands.

You gasp as it rockets to the back of the boat, directly toward the chart table and Georgina's head. The kit misses Georgina by inches, but she grabs it and gets to work cleaning up Jason's cut. Then you hear a scream from above.

It's Chelsea!

You race up to the deck to check on her. The wind and rain whip your face as you frantically search for her. Then you see a flash of her yellow jacket.

"Help me!" Chelsea cries out. "The backstay is loose!"

Oh, no! The backstay is an essential piece of wire that stops the mast from falling forward.

You start toward the stern but quickly lose your balance and nearly fall overboard. You forgot to hook on your safety harness. Chelsea isn't wearing hers either!

As you struggle in the wind to tether yourself to the boat, you yell out to Chelsea to do the same.

"No time!" she shouts back. "Come here *now*—or the mast will break!"

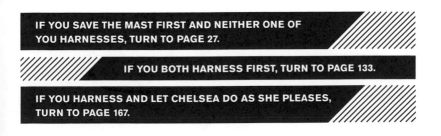

IF YOU SAVE THE MAST FIRST AND NEITHER ONE OF YOU HARNESSES, TURN TO PAGE 27.

IF YOU BOTH HARNESS FIRST, TURN TO PAGE 133.

IF YOU HARNESS AND LET CHELSEA DO AS SHE PLEASES, TURN TO PAGE 167.

You wait for Georgina to take a good look at that amazing fish. She swims toward it with you by her side, sharing her tank of air. The fish's distinctive stripes and spiny fins fan out over its entire body. Most other fish swim in schools, but this fish travels solo. It moves alongside a coral reef, then darts into a shadowy hole.

Georgina taps your shoulder, shakes out her hair, and makes roaring gestures. Then she points to the fish. Charades! You get it. That fish is a lionfish.

You've read about lionfish, but you had to learn so much to get ready for this journey that it's hard to match the correct fact with the correct sea creature. *What's special about it?* you wonder. Maybe if you get a better look, you'll remember.

You both move close against the reef, staying side by side since you are attached by the shared regulator. Through your scuba masks, you peer into the dark hole. The magnificent lionfish stares back.

Georgina is so entranced that she reaches her hand out toward it. "Ouch!" she gurgles. She recoils, and it's clear to you that she is in horrible pain. The lionfish stung her!

Tears well in her eyes. Her hand swells to three times its normal size. Now you recall that the lionfish is a member of the scorpionfish family, and its spines are poisonous. A sting from a lionfish is excruciating. Her hand must feel as if it's on fire.

You need to help Georgina, but how?

Georgina's pain grows more and more severe. The muscles in her hand and arm cramp up. She's overcome with light-headedness, and the regulator drops from her mouth. You reach for it but miss, since you are still attached to her tank. Seawater rushes into her mouth and she begins to sink, dragging you down with her. It's as if cement blocks are attached to your feet, pulling you to the bottom. The lionfish watches both of you drown from its reefy home. Georgina should have remembered her manners: look but don't touch!

THE END

"Jason is the skipper," you tell the others. "We need to respect the chain of command. If he thinks he's able to stay at the wheel, we need to trust his judgment."

"Give me some room!" Jason commands. "I can't steer with all of you breathing on top of me."

"Help me check the lines," Georgina says to you and Brandon, as David and Chelsea go below.

"I checked them yester—"

"Shh!" Georgina cuts off Brandon. "I want to stay close to Jason."

The three of you pretend to fix the ropes but really keep your eyes on Jason. The shallow ocean shimmers pale aqua in the sunshine. The winds blow strongly, whipping across the deck and filling the sails. Jason navigates expertly around the rocks and reefs, taking advantage of the high tide. He knows you are watching, and he seems more skilled exhausted than you are wide awake.

You watch the barren, jagged Australian coastline go by. Then you get company. A huge white bird lands on the deck. He enjoys the sunshine and free ride for an hour, then flies away.

Ugh! He left behind a present.

"Your turn to clean the deck!" Georgina says to you. Then she and Brandon laugh.

"Bird poop is good luck," Georgina says as she watches you scrub.

David comes back up, and he doesn't look as if he has good news. His brow is furrowed with concern. "The winds are changing, and so is the tide."

The gusty wind blows hard from the east, pushing the *Chronos II* closer and closer to a reef. You see the rocky ridge poking up from the clear rushing water. David tries unsuccessfully to judge by the breaking waves how long and deep it runs. Jason grits his teeth, as he steers, and sweat drips into his eyes.

You hurry to help Chelsea with the sails. Together, you all work to tack close to the reef. The plan is to change tacks at just the right moment to slip around the reef into another narrow passage. Timing is key. Darkness starts to fall, and the dim light makes maneuvering extra tricky. The crew gets ready to make the move on "three."

"One," Jason calls. "Two—"

Jason turns the wheel too fast and too soon. His judgment is off. CRASH! The hull hits the rocks. The only thing this overtired skipper should be counting is sheep. Sweet dreams! Your voyage has been put to bed.

THE END

I have a better chance of reaching David, you think.

David's diving rig has an extra regulator in case of an emergency. You start to swim to him, but he still has his back to you. Every time you get closer to him, he swims farther away from you.

Your chest really hurts now. Your lungs are empty. You're starting to feel dizzy.

Suddenly, David turns to you.

You point to your tank.

You feel yourself blacking out—it's too late.

But he reaches you in time. He passes his extra regulator to you. You take deep gulps, filling your lungs with oxygen.

You both head up to the surface, sharing his tank of air.

You make sure you swim slowly. You focus on exhaling. If you don't remember to exhale continuously, your lungs will burst.

Finally, you see sunlight cutting through the water's surface.

You made it!

⚓

It's time to leave Cairns.

Jason begins to pilot through the Torres Strait. It lies between Australia and Papua New Guinea, and it will take you to the Indian Ocean.

The strait is a sailor's nightmare. It's a maze of islands, over 200 of them. One strong wind can send you crashing into their rocky shores or stony coral reefs. Or you can run aground in the blink of an eye because the water is very shallow.

And that's the good news.

The bad news is Jason hasn't slept in a week. He keeps nodding off at the wheel, but he won't give up control of the boat.

Face it, you tell yourself. *You're dead in the water.*

"The winds are picking up," Georgina interrupts your thoughts.

Jason grips the wheel tighter.

The boat pitches back and forth.

Jason is taking the boat through a channel filled with reefs. Reefy and shallow.

Riiiiiip.

Everyone on deck gasps.

That's a sound you don't want to hear.

Riiiiiip. There it is again—the sound of your keel scraping against rock.

"Jason, if the hull splits, this game is over," Brandon says. "Give up the wheel. Now."

"Not happening," Jason says. "Unless you want to hit me in the head with a book."

Jason and Brandon haven't been getting along very well since the book accident.

"How about I take the wheel?" you say.

"Thanks, but I've got it," Jason says. "I'm the only one who can sail these kinds of waters."

BANG!

The keel smacks into a rock beneath the surface.

"I hope that wasn't the rudder," David says. He looks pale. "That sounded like the rudder to me."

"Get Chelsea," Brandon whispers to you. "Maybe she can convince Jason to give up the boat."

You find Chelsea below, sitting at the table, trimming her nails. Georgina is on the laptop, searching for the next window of good weather.

At the sound of your footsteps, Georgina looks up and lets out a shriek.

"What are you doing?" she shouts at Chelsea. Then she leaps across the cabin and snatches the nail clippers from her.

"Are you crazy?" Chelsea says. "Give that back to me."

"You'll ruin your nails with those," Georgina says, but you can tell that's not what she's really thinking.

"Chelsea, we need you on deck," you say. "You have to convince Jason to get some sleep."

Chelsea narrows her eyes at Georgina. "Okay," she says, following you up on deck.

"Jason, let someone else take the wheel for a while," Chelsea begs. "You have to rest."

"Not necessary," Jason says, his head nodding, heavy with fatigue.

"You can guide us through here," David whispers to you.

"If we leave Jason up there, this boat is history," Brandon agrees.

You're not sure what to do. Jason is more experienced than you are. Maybe he should stay at the helm in these tricky waters.

IF YOU TAKE OVER THE WHEEL, TURN TO PAGE 143.

IF YOU LEAVE JASON AT THE HELM, TURN TO PAGE 114.

It takes only four days to gather three other boats to form a flotilla.

"Mine will be the lead boat," announces a burly Egyptian man with thick, curly hair. "I've sailed this route many times."

Jason grumbles. He hates not being in charge.

"At least the other boats don't want to lead," you remark. One boat has two retirees, and the other has a French movie star and her entourage, who spend their time sun tanning.

The burly guy's name is Rami, and he's calling the shots. All four boats stay close, and you successfully make it through the Gulf of Aden and into the Red Sea. At one point, you spot a skiff filled with Somali men, but they veer away when they see you all together.

It's strange sailing so close to these people after all these months alone. The French boat is a floating party. Dance music thumps late into the night. The old people insist on constant radio contact, telling you all about their trip. You've heard their same stories twenty times now. And you just can't figure out Rami. He's always on his cell phone and never seems to sleep.

Together, your four boats sail the Gulf of Suez and approach the Suez Canal. The 118-mile canal connects the Red Sea to the Mediterranean Sea. Ships can travel in only one direction at a time because the canal is so narrow. Convoys of several ships are sent through together.

Canal officials tell you that every boat needs written approval from the Suez Canal Authority at least five days before crossing. The approval involves lots of paperwork and documents, along with health and immigration inspections—plus, all boats must hire a pilot to lead them through the canal. The *Chronos II* has none of that.

The French actress and the old couple already had their papers, and they leave to travel through the canal. David e-mails Mr. Houseman, but even with all his connections, it will take days. "Now we may not make it back in time," David points out. "Plus we already lost time waiting for the flotilla."

"I can help," Rami calls to everyone. "My cousin is a pilot. Plus I have friends who can make the approvals happen fast."

Excellent! Rami to the rescue. You were wrong to have been suspicious of him.

"My services come at a cost," Rami warns. "Give me your valuables. Laptops, music players, jewelry. I especially like those fancy watches you kids wear."

"I'm not giving you my stuff!" Georgina cries.

"Then you'll wait," Rami says. "My friends can make you wait here a long, long time. It could take weeks before you get through the canal."

"That's not fair," you protest. "You can't blackmail us."

Brandon and David agree.

"Can't I?" Rami sneers.

Jason gathers the crew into a huddle. "Maybe we should do it," he says. "Breaking the record is more important than some watches."

"How do we know Rami's legit?" Georgina asks. "What if we hand over our stuff and he doesn't deliver?"

"I refuse to pay this slimy guy a bribe," Chelsea declares.

"We can't let him bully us," Brandon says.

Jason nods. "You're right. We'll keep our watches and wait our turn."

TO WAIT FOR MR. HOUSEMAN TO GET APPROVALS, TURN TO PAGE 93.

"Over here!" you scream. "Hey! Here!" But the *Chronos II* sails in the opposite direction. Away from you.

Your legs paddle furiously as you try to keep your head above the surface. You start to swim toward the boat. *Pull, pull, kick, breathe.* You pause and shout to the yacht again. Your voice is a whisper in the howling wind, so it's back to swimming. *Pull, pull, kick, breathe.* You cut through one wave only to have another push you back.

You can't battle the waves head-on any longer. Changing course, you swim diagonally, avoiding the punishing pounding of the water. Your arms are no better than wet noodles. You raise your head to see if you are any closer to the yacht.

Oh, no! The *Chronos II* is a dot on the horizon. You've been swimming in the wrong direction.

Then a tightness grips your left side. A cramp. You bend over, trying to squeeze the jabbing pain away. It keeps coming. You roll your knees into your chest and grit your teeth. Then you start to sink. Twisting and tumbling, you lose sight of the surface.

You're headed to the bottom. And there you'll remain—in your watery grave under the sea.

THE END

You've watched enough *Shark Week* specials to know that your best hope is to fight back. If you swim and splash, the shark will only get more agitated and more aggressive.

Do you have what it takes to fight a shark? You sure hope so.

The shark glides toward you. Its massive head is within arm's reach. The time is now. Your plan is to gouge it in the eyes or punch it in the gills, its most sensitive spots. The nose is also sensitive, but it is way too close to those powerful jaws for your taste. Your fingers could get chomped off in one quick bite.

The shark is inches away now. Your heart hammers in your chest. You have only one chance. You go for the gills, pummeling with all your strength, blow after blow.

The shark recoils. It swims away from you, dazed and confused. You did it!

Now you swim like there's no tomorrow. And for you, there almost wasn't. The *Chronos II* is in sight, not too far away. The shark is no longer in sight, and you don't dare search for it. Hopefully it won't return for revenge.

You are almost back to the yacht. With a burst of energy, you pull your arms through the water . . . and then you feel your high-tech Chronos watch slip from your wrist. The momentum of your stroke flings it out of reach. It lands with a splash, and you can just make out the glint of the silver face as it bobs on the surface. It was a present from Jules Houseman Jr. Each crew member received one on the day you left California. It's stronger than steel, and you can read it underwater easily. It is incredible. Luckily, it also floats.

No one knows it, but you and Mr. Houseman have a secret connection. You plan to share it with the crew when the time is right. The watch is important to you—more important than the others realize. But now it is floating away on the waves.

IF YOU LET THE WATCH GO AND SWIM TO THE *CHRONOS II*, TURN TO PAGE 166.

IF YOU SWIM AFTER THE WATCH, TURN TO PAGE 67.

"It's a good-sized fish." You stare at its strange spines. "But I'm not sure what kind it is. I don't know how it will taste."

"It has to taste better than dirty worms," Brandon says. That's what Brandon calls the dehydrated spaghetti.

"Sorry. We have to throw it back," you say. "It's too dangerous to eat something we can't identify."

Your stomach grumbles, but you know it's the right thing to do. As you near the Panama Canal, you receive an unexpected treat. You finally catch your tuna. But the canal has another surprise for you—and this one is lethal.

Sailing into the Panama Canal is a nightmare. Worse than any storm you've been through. It's a major traffic lane for ships crossing between the Atlantic and Pacific Oceans. Huge ships.

You're thinking about this as Jason yells, "Ocean liner!" You look behind you. A big cruise ship is closing in and it wants to pass you.

Jason can't maneuver to escape in time. He grabs the VHF radio and contacts the ship. He's yelling.

You watch in horror as the liner gains on you.

Jason turns the wheel sharply. The radio flies out of his hand and soars overboard.

"Should we jump into the water before that ship crashes into us?" Chelsea asks.

"Don't think that's a good idea," David says, and he points into the water.

At the crocodiles staring back at you. Hungry crocodiles.

Just in the nick of time, the cruise ship slows down and a strong breeze carries you forward to safety.

You won't be jumping overboard, at least not today.

You meet with the Panama Canal Authority. There are lots of ships waiting their turn to travel through the canal. It takes forever, but they give you your time slot.

"That's not possible!" Jason shouts.

It takes only one day to pass through the canal—but the slot they have reserved for you is two weeks away. You can't wait that long. You'll lose the contest!

Jason begs the port captain. He tells him about the competition.

It works.

Two days later, a Panama boat pilot is assigned to your boat to guide you through the canal. This side of the canal is higher than sea level, so your boat needs to be raised up to sail through it. Your boat will enter a chamber, called a lock, where water enters and raises the boat.

Over fifty million gallons of water flood into the chamber. Your pulse quickens as the water rises, lifting the *Chronos II* up, up, up . . .

You travel through three sets of locks into Gatún Lake. As you sail across the lake, the scorching Panama sun beats down on you. Crocodiles snap their powerful jaws at you.

It's difficult to remain alert in the intense heat. You're tired, thirsty, and dizzy from the sun. But you have to be watchful.

You are approaching the chambers that will now lower you down to sea level into the Pacific Ocean.

The boat pilot helps Jason steer the yacht into the chamber. A tugboat helps guide you in.

Now you have to tie your boat to the chamber wall to stop the boat from moving as the water rushes out of the chamber into the Pacific Ocean.

"Throw the line," Jason and the pilot instruct you. You throw the line to a canal worker who will tie it to the wall for you.

Oh, no! The whole line falls into the water.

Quick! Do you jump in after it? Or is there time to look for another line onboard before the boat surges forward and crashes into the opposite wall?

IF YOU DECIDE TO JUMP IN FOR THE LINE, TURN TO PAGE 41.

IF YOU DECIDE TO LOOK FOR ANOTHER LINE ON BOARD, TURN TO PAGE 160.

You shake your head no. By sharing one tank, you'll run out of air twice as fast and, besides, that's a lionfish she wants to follow. Beautiful, sure. Dangerous, definitely. It stings with its venomous spikes.

On your way to the boat, the two of you swim by an intricate coral city. It teems with fish of every color and every shape. An enormous large-mouthed grouper swims close to check you out, then swims away, unimpressed. But you're impressed. In and around the reef, amazing creatures are busy swimming, eating, cleaning. You spot the most adorable clown fish, with its orange-and-white stripes.

Georgina yanks your arm away from what looks, at first, to be yellow-green seaweed.

Your eyes widen. It's not seaweed. It's fire coral! If you had touched it, you would've gotten a burning, itchy rash. Close call. You gesture thanks, and swim out of danger . . . and into the waiting tentacles of a pale-blue, bell-shaped box jellyfish. The nearly-transparent, gelatinous creature is the size of a basketball. It hits your leg with one of its sixty tentacles. The pain is indescribable. Your muscles tense and your body convulses. You forget to breathe. You forget everything except the intense, mind-numbing pain.

You're vaguely aware of arms pulling you up to the surface. You want to curl into a ball, but the pain won't allow you to move. It's as if your leg has been thrust into roaring flames. You try to form words, but you can't make a sound. You are hoisted up out of the water. You writhe on the deck of the boat.

"It was a box jellyfish," you hear Georgina explain.

"Oh, no! Box jellyfish are the most venomous marine creatures on earth," David cries.

"Every year people in Southeast Asia die from the stings of box jellyfish. The jellyfish wait around for something to bump into their poisonous tentacles," he explains.

"Gross!" Chelsea shrieks, staring at you. "There are still tentacles attached to your leg!"

Everyone peers at your shin.

"We need to pee on it," Brandon announces. "I had a snake bite last year while I was camping. We doused it with urine, and it got better. I can pee into a cup right now."

"Or we could try vinegar," Georgina suggests. "An old woman I met while sailing through the Philippines told me that apple cider vinegar cures stings. We only have white vinegar on board, but I bet that would work."

IF YOU POUR WHITE VINEGAR ON THE STING, GO TO PAGE 34.

IF YOU POUR URINE ON THE STING, GO TO PAGE 26.

"Chelsea!" you yell. The thundering waves drown out your cries. You scream louder. "Fasten your harness!"

A giant wave pounds the boat.

It hurls you and Chelsea through the air.

You harnessed in time, but did Chelsea?

Up, up, up . . . you both fly.

Maybe Chelsea was right, you think. Maybe you should have saved the boat first. Now you will both die anyway, the mast will crack, and the rest of the crew will be buried at sea.

The roiling ocean pounds the boat.

BAM! You come down hard, slamming onto the deck.

Chelsea does, too. She harnessed in time. You're both okay.

The wind beats at you both as you tighten the backstay, preventing the mast from falling forward and cracking.

By the time the storm leaves, you're exhausted—but you saved the boat and everyone on it.

Today Jason thinks the two of you are heroes. But that will soon change.

⚓

You've been at sea now for over two months. It's a quiet day on the water. You and Brandon decide to do some fishing.

"Hey," Brandon says as he casts his line. "I just remembered. You were going to tell me how you knew so much about the *Chronos I*—that yacht that sank."

"I, um . . ." you start, but Jason cuts you off.

"Brandon, how much longer to Cairns?" he shouts from the wheel.

Cairns is in far north Australia. It's the best place to start exploring the Great Barrier Reef. The reef is filled with coral gardens, thousands of different sea animals, and underwater canyons. You can't wait!

"We're about two weeks away," Brandon answers. Then he turns to you. "So, how do you know so much about that boat?"

You want to tell Brandon the truth, but now it's too late, you think.

"I read about it," you lie.

"Jules Jr. must be really, really rich. Building two yachts—the *Chronos I* and *II*—costs a lot of money," Brandon says.

"He's rich," you say. "But Jules Jr. built only *Chronos II*. His father, Jules Sr., built *Chronos I.*"

You tell Brandon more about the boat that went down. But there's something you don't tell him. Senior doesn't want Junior to succeed where he failed. Jules Sr. wants your boat to lose—and you wonder how far he'd go to stop you.

⚓

You've been at sea for two long months, so when the coastline of Cairns comes into view, you shout out with joy.

"Australia! We're here!" The rest of the crew joins you on deck to take in the shoreline's golden sandy beaches.

Cairns has something for everyone—beautiful beaches, amazing waterfalls, a fantastic rain forest—but you don't have time to see everything. What you and the crew want to do most is explore the Great Barrier Reef.

You put on your scuba gear and dive right in.

"Don't forget the camera!" Brandon throws the underwater camera to Georgina. He has volunteered to stay onboard.

The sea life here is incredible. The colors in this underwater world are astounding.

You swim among the stingrays and sea turtles. A seahorse glides by you. You explore an underwater canyon. Maybe you'll search for an ancient shipwreck. You've heard that the reef is littered with hundreds of them. It would be so cool to find one—and maybe a sunken treasure along with it!

You swim toward Georgina to see if she wants to explore with you—and gasp. It's not the barracuda that just passed that has taken your breath away. It's something much worse.

NO ONE SEES YOU.

YOU TAKE YOUR LAST BREATH. NOW WHAT DO YOU DO?

IF YOU TRY TO SWIM TO THE SURFACE AS FAST AS
YOU CAN, TURN TO PAGE 171.

IF YOU TRY MAKING YOUR WAY TO DAVID TO USE
HIS EXTRA REGULATOR, TURN TO PAGE 116.

The crew decides to go it alone. Only a few small boats sailed the IRTC with you, and no one wants to wait for more to appear. The Suez route was chosen for speed.

Full speed ahead!

The *Chronos II* leaves the IRTC early the next morning. Brandon hopes the gray mist of the dawn will help hide the yacht. Hours later, you stand on the deck and survey the flat, slate-blue ocean. For the first time in days, there are no other boats in sight. The *Chronos II* bobs all alone. That's when the distant rumble of an outboard motor breaks the silence.

"What's that?" you cry.

"I don't know," Brandon admits, squinting through the mist. "Chelsea! Can you see?"

"Over there! Starboard aft!" Chelsea yells down. She shimmied up the mast earlier to adjust the sail. "We have company!"

David hurries to your side with a pair of high-powered binoculars. He raises them to his eyes, then groans. "Not good." He hands them to you.

Two skiffs zoom across the water, kicking up a wake in their path. They are headed directly for you, as if zeroing in on a target. One veers off, then approaches from your port side. They have you trapped.

Each small boat holds five men, all brandishing rifles and machine guns. They yell in a language you don't understand, but that doesn't matter. You get the meaning.

They want to board your yacht.

Jason tries to veer to the left, but one of the boats cuts the *Chronos II* off. Your sailboat is no match for their motors. Or their guns.

One guy, with a black scarf wrapped around his head, stands and fires a warning shot with his rifle. The six of you huddle together as the bullet lands in the water. "We're in trouble," David whispers.

In seconds, several Somali pirates toss crude rope ladders onto your deck and scramble aboard. The man with the black scarf takes the wheel.

Georgina sobs and Jason's face grows red with fury as the men roughly push you below deck. They stink of sweat. Your mouths are duct-taped and your hands are bound tightly with twine. When Brandon tries to fight back, a pirate smashes the back of his head with the butt of his rifle. Brandon falls and hits his head on the floor. Blood trickles down his forehead.

You try to help him, but the pirate raises his gun at you.

The six of you squat in a corner for hours. Any movement angers the guard with the gun. You bite your lip against the pain of your cramping muscles. Your stomach knots in fear.

Jason catches your eye, then David's. He nods slightly toward Brandon's radio and computer. They're not far off. He raises his eyebrows, sending a message. The only hope is to get over there and try to send an SOS. Brandon is dazed from his injury, Georgina is still sobbing, and Chelsea just stares at the floor in shock. It's up to the three of you.

Jason grunts loudly. The guard tells him to shut up, but he groans even louder. The guard raises his gun to quiet Jason, but Jason shakes his head wildly. "What do you want?" the guard asks, his English heavily accented. He rips the tape from Jason's mouth.

"I need to go to the bathroom," Jason rasps.

The guard unties Jason's hands and watches him walk to the head. Jason is getting close to the equipment. Closer. Closer. You need to create a distraction now so he can use the radio!

You slam your legs on the floor, but at that moment several pirates hurry down the ladder. They grab Jason, just as he's inches away from the equipment. They drag you all up from the dark galley and onto a pier. You're driven to a damp hut with a dirt floor and told to wait.

The *Chronos II* decided to go it alone, and now you truly are alone. Your only choice is to wait until they find Mr. Houseman, and he agrees to pay the ransom. One million dollars for each of you.

Mr. Houseman spent a fortune on this voyage. You hope he has enough money left to buy back his crew.

THE END

Brandon is right. Jason is in no condition to pilot the boat safely.

"Okay. I'll do it," you say.

You approach Chelsea and Jason. You feel a little shaky. You've never steered a boat through islands and rocks and reefs—and you've never forced a skipper to surrender control of a boat.

"Jason, you have to go below and get some rest. You haven't slept in days. It's not safe to work this way." You reach out and place a reassuring hand on his shoulder. "You need some sleep."

Jason's glance darts to Chelsea. She nods in agreement. He glares at her. Then he knocks your hand from his shoulder. He looks over at Brandon and David. He can tell that no one is going to back down.

"Thanks for the support, everyone," he snaps. "You don't know what you're doing." He wants to argue more, but he doesn't. He heads below, and the tension that was building starts to ease. Everyone breathes a sigh of relief, except you—because you are now the one responsible for steering the boat through this treacherous path. Will you make it to the Indian Ocean—or will you bring down the yacht?

As you steer the boat, you try to remain calm.

You watch for anything rocky sticking up out of the water.

Brandon stands next to you at the helm, an extra pair of eyes on the lookout.

"The Torres Strait is doom and destruction for small boats like this one," Brandon tells you.

You wish he wouldn't talk. You're trying to concentrate. You've been holding your breath since you stepped up to the wheel, and Brandon is making you nervous.

"It takes down huge oil tankers, too," he goes on. "They collide with uncharted rocks. Takes them right out."

"Brandon . . ." you start.

"Then they come limping into port like sick puppies," he goes on. "All ripped up. Oil polluting the islands. A real disaster. Usually no one dies. Except back in . . ."

"Brandon! Stop! I'm trying to concentrate."

SCRAPE.

The bottom of the boat grazes the floor of the strait.

SCRAAAPE.

Louder this time. It sounds like you're slicing the hull.

Your stomach lurches.

SCRAAAAAPE.

The boat stops moving.

Your trip might be over—and it's all your fault.

As your heart sinks, a gust of wind blows out of the north. It rocks the boat—rocks it hard and shakes you loose.

You're doing great now.

You move forward slowly.

Then, without warning, the boat jerks backward—as if something yanked it back.

"What was that?" Brandon shouts.

You stare into the water and see it—a heavy rope, probably lost from a big ship, snaking through the water, wrapping around the keel of your ship. But the rope quickly unwinds itself, and the boat pitches forward.

Congratulations—you conquered the dreaded Torres Strait!

You continue to head into the Indian Ocean—and into another argument with the crew. This time it's about changing course—and once again the wrong choice could be deadly.

⚓

You've been at sea for nearly five months. Sailing the Indian Ocean has been unpredictable.

The winds are light. You're making very little progress. Then the water turns choppy. The boat slaps the waves as you sail right into them.

Chronos II creaks and groans and shakes, and makes all sorts of noises you've never heard before. With each thump on a wave, she sounds like she's cracking apart.

Jason is worried about the yacht and all the time you're losing in this lumpy sea. "I think we should change course," he says. "We can pick up speed if we sail through the Suez Canal—downwind—instead of going round the Cape of Good Hope—upwind."

You want to save time, too, but to travel the Suez, you have to sail through the Gulf of Aden—known as Pirate Alley!

Ships are attacked there daily.

Pirates seize boats and hold crews for ransom—if they don't shoot them first.

"Not every ship is attacked," Chelsea says when you mention this. "Maybe we should take our chances."

Jason agrees. "Around the Cape of Good Hope, we could hit ferocious winds and torrential rain. We could lose A LOT of time there—enough to lose the prize money."

You and the crew argue back and forth about which route to take. Finally, you all come to a decision.

IF YOU DECIDE TO TRY TO SAVE TIME AND TAKE THE SUEZ CANAL, TURN TO PAGE 43.

IF YOU REMAIN ON COURSE FOR THE CAPE OF GOOD HOPE, TURN TO PAGE 84.

Hit the shark? No way! This deadly fish is at least 10 feet long and weighs about 1,000 pounds. And its teeth are enormous!

I'm out of here, you think, and swim into action. Faster and faster you push yourself. Your legs kick violently, and your arms windmill through the water. The shark circles confidently. The yacht is still far off. Even if you screamed, no one would hear you. Your once-smooth strokes become jerky and frantic. Uh-oh. The more you flail, the more you attract the shark's attention.

The shark moves in again, circling even closer. It's so incredibly close you can see the dark stripes marking its body. A tiger shark. Knowing its name doesn't make you feel any better. In fact, it makes you feel worse. Tiger sharks are one of the most dangerous sharks to humans. They like to eat large prey—and you're just the right size! *Don't panic, don't panic,* you repeat to yourself, but your leg suddenly cramps. You flail in the water and hope the motion scares the shark away. But the frantic splashing only seems to make you more interesting to the hungry-looking tiger shark.

The shark's cold eyes are now gleaming with excitement. It stops circling. . . .

Blood trickles from your wound into the ocean, drawing the shark closer, eager for a taste. Its jaws open wide, exposing rows of razor-sharp teeth.

You try to massage the cramped muscle in your leg, but it doesn't help. The pain is paralyzing and you can't move, but at this point it doesn't really matter.

There's nowhere to go. No escape. Looks like the crew won't be eating with you tonight. You have a dinner date with a shark, and unfortunately you're the one on the menu.

THE END

"Stay right here," you say. "If you go down below, you'll feel worse."

"Okay," Brandon says. Holding the railing, he hangs his head down, waiting for the dizziness and nausea to end. But his knees start to buckle and he lets out a low, long moan.

"Look up, Brandon. Look out at the horizon," you tell him. "Looking down at the water will make you sicker."

Brandon follows your instructions, and the greenish color in his face slowly turns back to pink.

The storm quickly fades and so does Brandon's queasiness.

Even the most experienced sailors get seasick, and it's horrible when it hits. But you're glad that Brandon's problem was seasickness and not your story about *Chronos I.*

⚓

It's been about a month since you left Los Angeles. After that first squall, the yacht ran into a few more storms. A couple of them sent you off course, but Brandon is a great navigator. He re-charted your route, and you're back on track.

"Hey, look!" you shout. You're standing on deck—and you've spotted palm trees, lush green hills, and the top of a volcano rising up in the distance.

"Hawaii!"

Jason and David are on deck with you.

"Maybe while we're here, it will erupt," Jason says, pointing to the volcano. "Red-hot lava. Yes!"

David is busy worrying about the steering mechanism. He's always worrying about something on the boat. "It seems to be sticking," he says, not looking up.

You dash below to tell the others that you've reached land.

Chelsea stands at the sink, adding water to a dehydrated Tex-Mex beef casserole for lunch. "Freeze-dried meat," she groans.

Most of the food on board is dehydrated. That way it stays fresh, and it's very light so it doesn't weigh the boat down.

It ranges in taste from dust to mush.

But you're lucky to have a desalinator on board. It removes the salt from the seawater and turns it into fresh water.

Brandon and Georgina sit at the chart table studying upcoming weather forecasts. Brandon's shoes are on the table. One is filled with stale candy bars. The other is filled with the empty wrappers.

"You're such a slob," Georgina says as Brandon reaches into the shoe for some of the funky chocolate.

"Aloha!" you shout from the steps down to the cabin. "I have just what everyone here needs—one order of paradise. Come on up!"

⚓

"There are six islands out there," Jason says, pointing to a map.

"Which one is Hawaii?" Georgina asks.

"All six make up Hawaii," he explains. "We're going to stop at the one called the Big Island. David says we need a special part to repair the steering equipment. I know they'll have one there."

"Maybe we should radio ahead to make sure," David suggests.

"Don't have to," Jason says. "I've been to the sail shop on the Big Island. It's practically on the marina. They'll have it."

"We lost a little time in the storms," Brandon says. "We should call and make sure."

"Don't have to," Jason repeats. "They'll have it."

And that's that.

The way Jason makes decisions is getting on everyone's nerves. He never really considers what you or anyone else has to say. But you have to admit, he's been right about everything so far.

The *Chronos II* docks, and David hurries off to the sail shop for the part. Jason was right—the shop is near the harbor. But for the first time on your trip, Jason is wrong— they don't have the part you need.

The sail shop can get the gear in a few days. Chelsea buys some fresh fruit and veggies on the island. Then you and the crew do some quick sightseeing.

The Big Island is incredible. It has sandy beaches, looming mountains, a rain forest, and yes, an active volcano—but it's not spewing today.

You take the boat back out so Brandon can fish. You can't wait to have fresh fish for lunch and a real salad. No dusty dehydrated meals while you're here in Hawaii.

Brandon throws a line out—and quickly reels in one snapper after another. He cooks them for the crew, and you all eat together on deck. There's pineapple and strawberries for dessert, but Brandon decides to eat a banana.

As he lifts it to his mouth Georgina leaps across the deck, snatches it from him, and throws it overboard.

"Hey!" Brandon says. "Why did you do that?"

"It was rotten," Georgina says.

"It didn't look rotten," Brandon says.

You could be wrong, but it looked perfectly ripe to you. *Strange,* you think.

After lunch, Brandon and David sew up a hole in the jib. Jason pilots the yacht closer to shore so you, Chelsea, and Georgina can snorkel.

"Aren't you going to take that necklace off?" Georgina points to Chelsea's gold necklace.

"Why?" Chelsea asks. "I never take it off."

"Nothing shiny in the water, remember?" Georgina says. "It can attract sharks."

"You worry too much," Chelsea says.

Georgina turns to you. "Tell her to take it off."

You don't want to get dragged into their argument. In fact, after spending all these weeks in tight quarters, you'd like a little time alone.

IF YOU DECIDE TO SNORKEL BY YOURSELF, TURN TO PAGE 80.

IF YOU DECIDE TO SNORKEL WITH CHELSEA AND GEORGINA, TURN TO PAGE 57.

Up and over, that's the plan. You'll use your body as a surfboard, straightening yourself out to become as streamlined as possible. The next big swell forms. It's heading directly for you. You have only seconds to launch your body over the towering wall of water.

Three . . .

Two . . .

Oh, no! Your timing is off. You aren't in the right position, and you can't get in front of the wave fast enough.

One . . . CRASH!

Water pummels you. You tumble about like a dirty sock in a washing machine. Salt water pours into your lungs, into your ears, into your eyes. The surface is nowhere in sight. Darkness envelops you.

Instead of going over, you are going down . . .

down . . .

down . . .

down to the bottom of the sea.

THE END

"Abandon ship!" you cry.

"Why wait until the boat drags us down to the bottom of the ocean?" Brandon adds. "Let's get out of here!"

You and Brandon remove the lashing wires and dislodge the bright-orange life raft, then lower it into the swirling sea. Georgina gathers the life jackets. David grabs the prepacked emergency grab bag.

You all work quickly and are secured in the life raft in less than a minute.

"Okay, we're all in safely. Let's get out of here," Jason says as he pulls the release cord and the raft is set adrift.

Huddling together, you toss about on the swollen sea. Darkness blankets the raft. In the dead of night you can't even see your hands.

But you can sure feel Georgina's cold feet on your legs. The six of you are squeezed shoulder to shoulder with no room to spare. The wind whips Chelsea's long hair into your face, and Brandon keeps elbowing you in the side. Together you ride out the storm.

By the next morning the ocean has settled and the sun is out. You can see the *Chronos II*, but barely. It's now just a speck on the horizon—and it's upright!

You made the wrong choice abandoning the boat.

IF YOU RAISE THE CANOPY, TURN TO PAGE 56.

IF YOU KEEP THE CANOPY DOWN, TURN TO PAGE 99.

You search frantically for another line to throw. No way are you risking the jaws of a hungry crocodile.

"Here, take this!" Georgina throws you a rope.

"You can't use that!" the pilot yells. "It's not heavy enough."

"Oh, no!" Georgina realizes her mistake. "He's right. That rope is too thin. It's half the width it should be."

"It doesn't matter," David says. "It's just as strong as the thicker ones. Use it! Use it!"

The boat is veering away from the lock wall. It has to be tied to keep it under control.

You turn to the Panama pilot. Will he let you use it?

Yes! He gives you the go-ahead.

You secure the boat, and Jason and the pilot enter the lock safely.

You sail to the ocean under the Bridge of the Americas. The Panama pilot returns control of the boat to Jason.

Welcome to the Pacific!

A pod of dolphins appears portside. There must be at least thirty of them. They try to get close to the boat, as if they're playing a game of tag with you. You watch as they whistle and click and ride the waves alongside the yacht.

The crew is on deck enjoying the dolphin show.

You rush below to get a camera.

You rifle through a bag that looks just like yours—and realize it's not when you come up with Georgina's diary. You can't help yourself. You have to peek inside. You scan the first page—and, suddenly, you understand everything:

My stupid brother wished me good luck today as the boat took off. He knows saying "good luck" to someone on a boat brings bad luck. He knows how superstitious I am. He did it on purpose. Sorry, but I had to punch him in the nose and make him bleed. Blood reverses the curse.

There are other entries about bad luck:

—Had to snatch Brandon's banana from him and throw it overboard. He probably thought I was nuts, but bananas on board are bad luck.

—I'm sure Chelsea hates me, but you can't cut your nails or hair onboard ship. Definitely bad luck.

—What was Jason thinking, bringing a BLACK bag on the boat?!? Black is the color of death. Totally BAD luck. Good thing no one saw me toss it overboard.

—This crew doesn't have a clue about bad luck. I'm working hard, keeping them safe.

You close the diary. You don't want to be caught snooping, but you're glad you did. Georgina isn't crazy—she's just very superstitious, like a lot of sailors you know.

You feel much better about her. But how will she and the crew feel about you when they learn your secret?

⚓

It's a week later, and you're all on deck, talking about the wind. There hasn't been much of it, sailing has been slow, and time is running out.

"With a little luck, we can still make it on schedule," Jason says, and Brandon agrees, although they both look tense.

At the mention of the word *luck*, Georgina's attention sharpens.

You hope she has some good luck charms stowed away, because you're gazing out to the horizon and you can't believe what you see.

A dark blotch. It's a squall. It's miles wide—and it's coming at you, fast!

The sky turns black, the wind picks up. A bolt of lightning lights up the sky. You don't want to be the tallest object in the ocean when lightning strikes, but you are.

Chelsea and Brandon start to trim the sails. You and David clean off the deck.

"Watch out!" Chelsea screams at you.

But it's too late.

THE HIGH WINDS CARRY THE BOAT FAR AWAY FROM YOU.

NO ONE CAN SPOT YOU.

IF YOU STAY WHERE YOU ARE, TURN TO PAGE 175.

IF YOU START SWIMMING TOWARD THE BOAT, TURN TO PAGE 123.

You start to swim back to the yacht. The watch is just a fancy toy, you tell yourself. It's not worth drowning or risking another shark attack. The shark could still be nearby. Besides, if you make it to California and win the challenge, you're sure you can ask Mr. Houseman for another one.

Lost in your thoughts, you swim mechanically back to the yacht. You wish you weren't out here alone. You can hear your crewmates in your mind, encouraging you to swim on. Chelsea, especially, would insist that you not give up. But the waves are growing higher and stronger, making it more difficult to keep up your good form. One minute they toss you up like a rag doll. The next, they force you under and hold you there.

Up. Down. Up. Down.

The water slams against your body, rushing up your nose and down your throat. The salty liquid makes you gag. Coughing and sputtering, you desperately try to battle forward into the waves. How are you going to fight your way through this treacherous sea? Every stroke you take is like slamming yourself into a concrete wall. You need to make a choice.

IF YOU TRY TO LAUNCH YOURSELF OVER THE CRESTS OF THE WAVES, TURN TO PAGE 156.

  IF YOU TRY TO SWIM UNDER THE WAVES, TURN TO PAGE 69.

"No!" you cry to Chelsea. "Safety first." You clip your harness onto the wire line running around the boat, then give it a tug to test its strength.

"Chelsea, clip on!" you plead with her again over the howling wind.

"Later!" She turns her back, pushing away the wet strands of hair that slap across her face. Then she leans forward and grasps the backstay.

You watch as she secures it, ensuring that the mast doesn't crack. You feel silly, swaying in the wind and rain, as Chelsea does all the work.

She whirls around, hands on her hips. "Big help you were," she accuses.

"Chelsea—" You grab onto her arm as the boat pitches violently. You both tumble across the deck, banging your knees and elbows. "Let's go below," you tell her. "We've got to get out of this storm."

"No. I'm going to check all the lines." Chelsea's eyes blaze with a fierce determination.

"I'll help," you insist. You wouldn't leave her alone in a storm. "We'll get it done faster together."

"Let go of me!" Chelsea cries.

You squint through the puddles collecting in your eyes. The rain is coming at you sideways. You glance down. You're still gripping Chelsea's arm.

"Let go!" she repeats and wriggles to free herself.

Slowly, you release your hand. At that moment, a terrifying wave crashes over the boat The foaming water scoops both of you in its rush across the deck. Your safety harness tightens, cutting through your clothes and into your skin. The cord groans against the weight of the water.

The wave retreats into the sea. You're splayed on your stomach on deck, gasping for breath, but you're still attached to the boat by your harness.

But Chelsea . . . where is Chelsea?

You scan the vast ocean for her. There's no sign of her. You scream for help. But there's nothing anyone can do. She wasn't harnessed in. You didn't insist. The only thing you did was let her go. And now she is gone for good.

THE END

"This way!" you cry, pulling Chelsea as you race toward the stern. The shadow of the mast looms and you quickly realize your mistake. "No, no! Turn around!" you yell. You try to push Chelsea back the way you came.

Too late.

The mast plunges, clipping your backs as it falls. Intense pain shoots down your side, and you fear you've broken a rib. You want to cry out, but before you can, you are tumbling off the boat. In that instant, you realize why clipping on the safety harness would have been a much better choice.

You splash into the inky black water. Chelsea tumbles overboard as well. Your thoughts are a jumble as the waves toss you about. Heart racing, you try to find the boat. It's not far off. You see the silhouettes of your crewmates now on deck. They are yelling, but it is difficult to hear them in the wind and rain.

The water begins to wrap its frigid fingers around you. At least you and Chelsea have life jackets on. You are thankful you remembered that safety warning, at least.

"Here! Here! I'm here!" you try to yell. Every breath slices painfully through your aching ribcage.

You raise your arms above your head. You have to make sure they see you.

But how? you wonder. The sky and ocean blend together in a sheet of blackness. You can't even see Chelsea anymore. You call out to her, but she doesn't answer. You train your eyes on the boat. The crew is using the motor, only to be employed in life-and-death emergencies, to head . . . where? It's definitely not to you.

Then you spot the tiny light. Chelsea has enabled the flashlight and emergency locator beacon on her life jacket. Her exact location is being transmitted via GPS to the boat's computer and to Mr. Houseman's warm, cozy offices on dry land.

You need to turn yours on, too. With stiff fingers, you press the button.

No light.

You press it again. Nothing.

You slap at it. Hit it. You try to turn it on every which way. Still nothing. Your beacon is defective.

Rescue will come for Chelsea, but rescues take time, especially out in the frigid open ocean. And time is your enemy. Your body is losing heat fast. Hypothermia is setting in. When the crew finally circles about in the darkness, searching for you, you will have already met a very watery . . .

THE END

All you can think about is air. You begin to swim to the surface as fast as you can. Your flippers flutter rapidly as you kick, pushing yourself up, up, up through the sea.

You watch your tank's pressure gauge drop sickeningly fast. *Swim, swim!* you push yourself, desperate to escape. The aqua-green water swirls around you, making you dizzy. Hundreds of tiny fish dart about. It becomes increasingly difficult to draw in air. Your head pounds with an incredible pressure. Nausea overwhelms you, and for a moment, you stop kicking. Stop swimming.

No, no, don't do that, you tell yourself, cringing at the excruciating pain deep in your shoulders and knees.

Then some piece of information buried in your brain resurfaces. You remember what you learned in all those classes to become a certified scuba diver. If you ascend too quickly, you'll get decompression sickness, also called the bends. Nitrogen gas bubbles will form inside your body tissue, causing possible paralysis, unconsciousness, or even death.

Now what? Glancing once again at your tank gauge, you can't believe what you see. *It's wrong,* you tell yourself. *It's broken. It has to be.*

It's not. Time to face facts—you've gotten in too deep!

You are so grateful. Georgina reacted immediately, initiating the low-on-air procedure and sharing her octopus regulator. She saved your life and you owe her—big time.

Together, you begin to ascend at a controlled speed with the air hose connecting both of you to her tank. Then Georgina stops swimming, forcing you to halt, too. You raise your hands to ask, "What's wrong?" She points to a beautiful, exotic fish swimming. It has bold stripes, showy fins, and jazzy spikes. Georgina has a thing for fish. She's told you about the two enormous aquariums she has in her bedroom back home.

You nod and motion to continue upward. You don't want to jinx your luck. The air in Georgina's tank will run out twice as fast with two people breathing it. When and if that happens, you want to be up by the boat—not 20,000 leagues under the sea!

Georgina won't go. She's mesmerized by the fish. She holds up a finger to say "wait a minute." You're torn. You owe Georgina, and she's only asking for a minute to see an amazing fish. But, then again, a minute can make all the difference if you're gasping for air.

IF YOU ALLOW GEORGINA THE TIME TO EXPLORE, TURN TO PAGE 112.

IF YOU MAKE HER RETURN IMMEDIATELY TO THE BOAT, TURN TO PAGE 130.

You wave your arms wildly. "Over here! I'm over here!" you scream.

They still have their backs to you, searching over the wrong side of the boat.

No one hears you.

The storm is overhead. The waves churn in the wind. The rain beats down on you.

You try to tread water calmly. But it's hard to stay on top of the waves in the storm.

They'll keep searching, you tell yourself. *They'll keep searching until they find me.*

We're so close to home. So close to winning, you think. How could this have happened? You've been at sea for over eight months. You're about three weeks away from sailing victoriously into port and claiming the prize.

"I'm over here!" you yell out, frustrated and frightened.

But no one can hear you over the gusting wind.

You don't want to drown. Conserve your strength, you tell yourself.

Your shoes are weighing you down. You kick them off. The waves pound you. It's time to make a flotation device.

You struggle to keep your head above water as you wriggle out of your pants. You tie each leg with a double knot. Then you swing the pants over your head to fill them with air.

You tie off the waist—and you have it—a life preserver! Your pants help keep you afloat in the stormy sea.

A bolt of lightning knifes the sky. You've never been this scared in your life.

But the storm starts to pass. Your panic eases. *Everything is going to be okay*, you think.

Then you feel it.

The fin of a fish—a big fish—swipes your bare legs. Your heart begins hammering in your chest.

The boat turns around. It's headed in your direction.

The fin brushes against your bare feet now.

Hurry! you think. *Please, hurry!*

You wave like crazy, trying to get the crew's attention.

"We see you!" they all wave back and shout.

"Hurry! Shark!" you holler.

They work furiously, unfurling the sails. Getting to you as quickly as possible.

The fish bumps you. Taunts you.

The boat is here. David throws you a life preserver and a rope. As you struggle to get onboard, the fish leaps out of the water after you. You gasp.

Georgina watches, wide-eyed—and laughs.

It's a dolphin.

"Dolphins are good luck," she says. "Did you know that?"

"I do now," you say.

⚓

The sun shines in the crystal-blue cloudless sky. The breeze fills the sails of the *Chronos II* as she skips over the waves up the California coast.

It's day 284 of your journey. Two-and-a-half weeks ago you were nearly dead in the water. But you're here.

You made it.

In less than one hour, you will sail into the same port you left more than nine months ago. You can't wait to see your family. You are so proud of what you and your crewmates have accomplished. You sailed around the world—and lived to tell the tale!

As the boat enters the harbor, you can't believe what you see.

You make your way to the stage set up for your arrival. The crowd crushes you with hugs.

Jules Houseman Jr. greets you on stage and takes the microphone. "You are all exceptional, and I am so proud of your incredible accomplishment." He smiles broadly, congratulating each of you with a handshake and an envelope containing your prize money.

You know that your envelope is empty, but you take it anyway and smile. "Thank you, Uncle Jules," you say.

"*Uncle* Jules?" Brandon says. The other crew members glare at you in shock.

"I passed the same test you did to sail on the *Chronos II*, but I thought if you knew who I was, you wouldn't treat me like one of the crew," you explain.

You didn't take this challenge for the money, you took it to sail and conquer the sea. And the crew will forgive you when they realize you've given them your share of the prize.

Right now, there are smiles all around because you all earned the right to say you sailed the deadly seas—and won!

CONGRATULATIONS! YOU'VE ACHIEVED . . .

THE ULTIMATE SUCCESS

THE END!

"It's difficult to sail through fog without radar, but let's keep going. We took Cape Horn to save time," Jason reminds everyone. "We shouldn't stop now."

Jason carefully, slowly navigates the boat with Brandon's help. Below, David works on getting the navigation equipment back online. The rest of you are on lookout duty.

The fog is icy and it makes you shiver. You try to peer through it, searching for nearby obstacles, the hint of a rock or the shadow of another boat. You don't see anything, but you know you can't trust your eyes. An object could be right in front of you—but in this fog, invisible at the same time.

You can't trust your ears either. Fog has a funny way of bending sound so you can't tell where a noise or a voice is coming from. If your VHF radio were working, you'd be monitoring vessel traffic and reporting on your own position to the nearby boats. But David is still working on a fix. He can't figure out why all your equipment went down at once. In the meantime, the best you can do is sound your foghorn to warn other boats that you're here.

The *Chronos II* snakes through the sharp rocks along the shoreline. It's amazing that Jason can maintain this kind of control over the boat, you're thinking—and then it happens. You hear a sickening squeal.

"What's that?" Georgina cries out as a strong jolt sends her flying right into you.

"We've hit bottom," you say.

The yacht has run aground along the shore of a deserted island. You get out to see where, exactly, you've landed, and you realize that you're stuck—but not alone.

A group of Magellanic penguins and a colony of seals welcome you to your new home. Be nice to them—you'll be rescued, but not for a long, long time.

THE END

"Go down below," you tell Brandon. He listens to your advice.

You grip the mast as the rain pummels you and the waves crash onto the deck. The *Chronos II* swirls around the same way your plastic boats used to when the bathtub drain was unplugged.

Down below, Brandon's stomach is swirling, too. He soon returns, and you gape at the color of his face. It is a terrible sickly green. He races to the edge and barfs. Brandon clutches the rail, but each crashing wave nearly sends him flying.

It takes every ounce of energy for you to keep on your feet. Your knuckles are white from the iron grip you have on the mast. The next wave pitches the boat nearly sideways. You scream as Brandon, not hooked into his safety harness, is swept into the churning ocean. The pounding waves drown out your cries.

Brandon is gone. Now your stomach churns, too. Losing your crewmate is enough to make the heartiest sailor sick.

THE END

"There's a small cove," Jason says, pointing out a place to drop anchor for the night. "By tomorrow afternoon, the fog should lift, and we'll be able to find our way out of this maze."

"And maybe our navigation equipment will be back online," Chelsea says, glancing at David.

"I'm working on it," David says, "but I'm not having much luck yet."

You drop anchor, and everyone tries to relax a little. It's hard to unwind. Even in the cove, huge waves rock the boat, and the wind never stops blowing. After dinner, David suggests a game of Scrabble. He takes out the board game and makes the first word—GHOST.

Georgina shudders. "I was just thinking about ghosts," she says. "Do you think Cape Horn is haunted by the ghosts of the sailors who died here?"

"Only on foggy nights," Brandon says.

"Only on foggy nights?" Georgina repeats.

"Yes," Brandon says. "They rise from their watery graves because they know they can hide in the mist. Then they wait for a passing ship. They sneak on board, kill the crew, and take over the boat."

"Really?" Now there's a tremble in Georgina's voice.

"No. Not really," Jason says. "Brandon is making this stuff up."

"Hey, you never know." Brandon shrugs his shoulders.

"I don't believe in gho—" Chelsea starts, but stops at the sound of an eerie howl outside.

"It's just the wind," you say, but a shiver runs down your spine.

The boat starts to rock hard, much harder than before. And the wind is really gusting now. Something is definitely not right.

"I think someone should go up on deck and check things out," David says.

You and Jason stand at the same time. "We'll both go," Jason says. He climbs on deck first. "Oh, no!" he cries out. "I don't believe this."

Your heart starts to pound. "What's wrong?" you ask. But you're on deck now and you can see for yourself. The anchor has come loose. You've been drifting in the violent waves toward another boat, and you are going to . . . CRASH!

THE END

"Let's cook it for dinner," Brandon says.

"I don't know. It's kind of weird looking," you say.

"You're kinda weird looking, but we kept you." Brandon laughs. "This fish is going to taste awesome. Trust me."

⚓

At dinner, everyone cleans their plates and talk soon turns to the next part of your journey—traveling through the Panama Canal.

"We have to watch out for crocodiles there," David says—and Chelsea lets out a long moan.

"Did we finally find something Chelsea is afraid of?" Georgina laughs. But soon Georgina is moaning too—along with everyone else. You all feel like vomiting, your faces are strangely numb, and you're dizzy.

"What kind of fish was that?" Jason asks.

"A brown, spiky, porcupine-y fish," Brandon says.

"Ohhh," Jason groans. "Don't you know that you're not supposed to eat a fish you can't identify?"

Oh, well. You and the crew will have plenty of time to learn about that fish—in the hospital in Venezuela where you go to recover from food poisoning and huge disappointment. Your trip is done.

THE END

EXPEDITION FILE:
DEADLY SEAS

To: My Dream Team Crew
From: Mr. Jules Houseman Jr.
Re: The Sail Around the World

This Expedition File contains maps, diagrams, safety tips, and other life-saving information. Please review it carefully before you set sail.

You were all chosen for your remarkable seaworthy abilities, but out in the open water when the wind is gusting and the waves are breaking, preparation is extremely important. Decisions must often be made in a split second. I am relying on you to make the right ones.

I trust your team will circumnavigate the globe safely and return home winners. Good luck!

Ahoy!
Jules Houseman Jr.
President and Founder of Chronos Watch Company

Return

Home

Menu

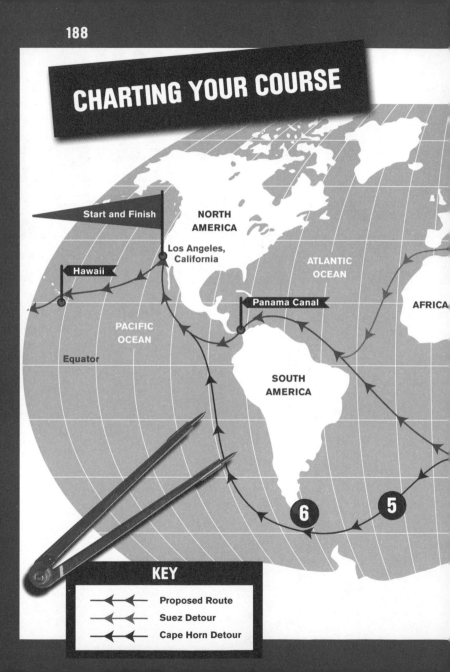

1 The Great Barrier Reef
Longest reef in the world!

2 Torres Strait
A sailor's nightmare! Lots of reefs, islands, and boat-mangling obstacles.

3 Cape of Good Hope
The ghost ship *The Flying Dutchman* haunts these waters. If you spot the phantom ship, you are headed for doom!

EUROPE

Suez Canal

ASIA

PACIFIC OCEAN

INDIAN OCEAN

AUSTRALIA

SOUTHERN OCEAN

ANTARCTICA

4 Gulf of Aden
Called "Pirate Alley."

5 Southern Ocean
Miles and miles of open water with no land in sight! Watch out for icebergs!

6 Cape Horn
Super-dangerous seas!
Called "the sailors' graveyard."

THE CHRONOS II

Jules Houseman instructed his boat builders to design the "fiercest boat around" when they built the *Chronos II*. The boat you will sail on is a 40-foot racing yacht. It has a custom fiberglass hull and a carbon-fiber mast.

Boom: The horizontal pole that extends from the bottom of the mast. Adjusting the boom forward or back changes the position of the mainsail, which allows the boat to use wind power to move forward.

Deck: The outside part of the boat that you walk on.

Hull: The body of the boat.

Keel: A heavy finlike piece that sticks out from the bottom of the hull. The keel stops the boat from tipping over.

Mainsail: The larger sail.

Jib: The smaller, front sail.

Mast: The main pole that holds up the sails.

Rig: The mast, boom, and a system of wires called the "running rigging."

Rudder: Located beneath the boat, the rudder is a flat piece of wood, fiberglass, or metal that is used to steer. The rudder is controlled with a tiller or a wheel on board the boat.

Stay: A large wire that supports the mast.

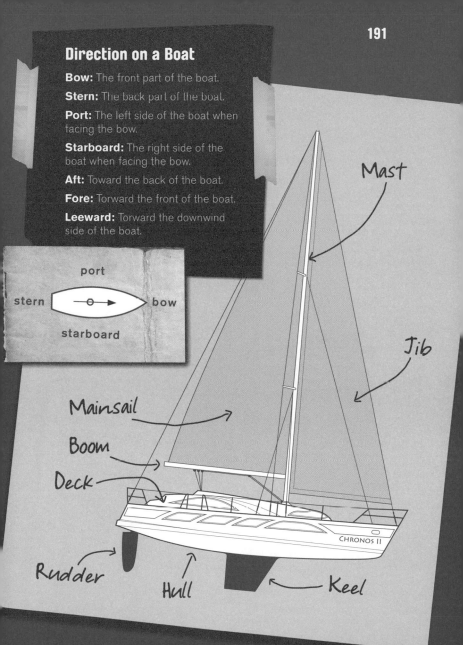

Direction on a Boat

Bow: The front part of the boat.

Stern: The back part of the boat.

Port: The left side of the boat when facing the bow.

Starboard: The right side of the boat when facing the bow.

Aft: Toward the back of the boat.

Fore: Toward the front of the boat.

Leeward: Toward the downwind side of the boat.

port

stern → bow

starboard

Mast

Jib

Mainsail

Boom

Deck

Rudder

Hull

Keel

CHRONOS II

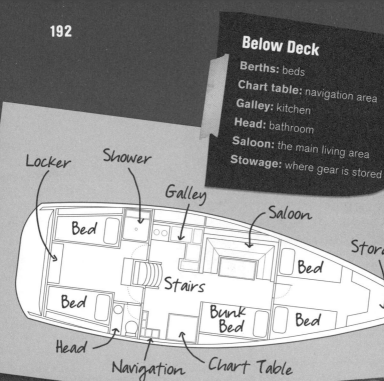

Below Deck

Berths: beds
Chart table: navigation area
Galley: kitchen
Head: bathroom
Saloon: the main living area
Stowage: where gear is stored

Locker
Shower
Galley
Saloon
Storage
Bed
Bed
Bed
Stairs
Bunk Bed
Bed
Head
Navigation
Chart Table

Sailing Terms

Tacking: Turning the bow of the boat through the wind so that the wind changes from one side of the boat to the other side.

Jibing: Turning the stern of the boat through the wind so that the wind changes from one side of the boat to the other side.

Nautical mile: The unit of measure for distance at sea used by all nations. It is based on the circumference of Earth. A nautical mile equals 1.85 kilometers or 1.15 miles.

Knot: The unit of measure for speed at sea. If you are traveling at a speed of 1 nautical mile per hour, you are traveling at a speed of 1 knot, which is 1.15 miles per hour on land.

Three Important Sailing Knots

Sailors use ropes (called lines) to haul sails, secure rigging, raise and lower anchors, and a variety of other jobs. Since lines must stay secure in strong winds and when wet, knowing how to tie strong knots is important. Here are three important knots you may need on your journey.

1. The Reef Knot: A reef knot is used to tie together two lines that have the same thickness. It is the perfect knot for tying, or reefing, the mainsail to the boom.

2. The Bowline: The bowline, sometimes called the "king of knots," is best used when docking. The loop can be thrown over a docking post, called a bollard.

3. Round Turn and Two Half-Hitches: This knot is used to attach a line directly to a pole or a ring.

Shark Attack!

Even though shark attacks are extremely rare, you may find yourself face-to-jaws with this deadly ocean predator. Be prepared by knowing your sharks. The three types responsible for most human attacks are the great white shark, the tiger shark, and the bull shark.

How to Avoid an Attack:

- Always swim with a buddy.

- Don't swim at dawn, dusk, or at night. Sharks don't have good eyesight, so when it's dark, you look like dinner.

- Stay away from large groups of fish, seals, or sea lions. They are sharks' favorite food.

- If you cut yourself in the water, get out! Blood attracts sharks.

- Sharks like shiny jewelry. It looks like fish scales to them.

If you see a shark approaching . . . Stay still and upright. Thrashing and splashing will excite the shark.

If the shark is zigzagging . . . It's looking for angles to attack from. Back up against a reef, a boat, or go back-to-back with your swimming buddy.

If the shark is circling . . . Watch out! It's about to zoom in for the attack.

If the shark takes hold of you . . . Fight! Giving up will not change the shark's mind about eating you. If there is floating wood nearby or you have a snorkel, use it as a weapon. If not, use your fists. Hit the eyes, gills, or nose. They are the shark's most sensitive parts. Many short, hard jabs are better than one big punch.

Return

The Panama Canal

Before 1914, if sailors wanted to reach the Atlantic Ocean from the Pacific Ocean or vice versa, they had to sail around the tip of South America. Then the Panama Canal was built across the narrowest part of Central America. A canal is a man-made channel for water—it's kind of like a new river where one never existed. Because the Pacific Ocean's water level is higher than the Atlantic and the land across Panama is not level, an amazing series of artificial lakes and locks were built to raise or lower boats on their journey across.

How a lock works

1. The gates open and a boat moves in.

2. The gates close, and water is let into or out of the chamber, depending on the direction the boat's heading. Every boat must be secured to the canal wall on both sides using four ropes so it doesn't capsize.

3. Water levels are equalized then the boat moves out.

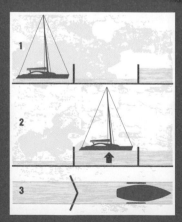

Caribbean
Sea

Limón
Bay

Gatún
Locks

Gatún
Dam

Gatún
Lake

Nicaragua

Caribbean Sea

Panama Canal

Costa
Rica

Pacific Ocean

PANAMA

Colombia

Gaillard
(Culebra) Cut

Miraflores
Lake

Pedro Miguel
Locks

PANAMA
CITY

Miraflores
Locks

PANAMA

Bay of
Panama

Return

Home

Menu

Fish That Will Kill You or Make You Really, Really Sick

There is no easy way to tell which fish are poisonous to eat and which fish will attack or sting you with deadly venom. Many poisonous fish are found in shallow water around reefs and lagoons. If you catch a fish you can't identify, it's best not to eat it, especially if it has a boxy or round body and spikes.

Puffer fish (also called blowfish, globefish or swellfish) This cute fish blows up like a spiky balloon to scare predators and is filled with a deadly poison called tetrodotoxin. If you eat a lot of this poison, it paralyzes your muscles and you will die within hours.

Lionfish If a lionfish punctures you with its sharp spines, it will inject a poison that causes intense pain, difficulty breathing, and paralysis.

Box jellyfish This venomous creature kills more people in Australian waters every year than sharks and crocodiles combined. Box jellyfish aren't aggressive, but swimmers bump into them by accident. If their tentacles touch your body, their poison seeps into your bloodstream and can stop your heart and lungs.

What to Do If Your Scuba Tank Runs Out of Air

 Do not panic.

 Signal to your fellow divers.
Make the "out-of-air" signal by slashing
your hand across your throat.

 Share a regulator if one is available.

If someone comes to help you, see if he or she has an extra
regulator so you can share his or her tank of air.

 Don't give up.

If no one can help you, keep your regulator in your mouth as
you swim to the surface. Air may expand in the tank, giving
you more air than expected. Look straight up, so you don't
accidentally inhale water.

 Swim to the surface slowly.

With the regulator still in your mouth, inhale and exhale
(breathe out) slowly as you swim upward. You must keep
exhaling. Exhaling releases the air in your lungs. WARNING:
If you do not exhale continuously, your lungs will burst!

How to Survive Adrift at Sea

 Stay on your boat as long as possible before you get into a life raft.

Your best chance of survival is on your boat, even if it can no longer sail. Only get into the life raft if the boat is sinking.

2 **Make sure you grab your prepacked "grab bag."**

Inside should be: warm, dry clothes; blanket; hat; canned food; handheld VHF radio; handheld GPS; compass; jugs of drinking water; flashlight with extra batteries; handheld flares; fishing gear.

3 **Bring fresh water!**

A person can die in as little as two days without fresh water. Do not drink seawater because the salt in it will dehydrate you.

4 **If you are in cold weather or cold water, get warm.**

Your biggest danger is dying of hypothermia. Hypothermia is when the body gets cold and loses heat faster than it can make it. Put on dry clothes and blankets and stay out of the water.

Protect yourself from the sun.

If your life raft has a canopy, put it up. Wear a hat, long sleeves, and pants if you have them. Cover your eyes with sunglasses or fabric.

Find food.

You should have fishing gear in your grab bag. If not, you can make a hook out of an aluminum can or a piece of wire.

Try to get to land only if you know where it is.

Most rafts include small paddles, but life rafts are not easy to steer. Do not exhaust yourself, especially if you don't know where you are going.

If you see a plane or boat, try to signal it.

Use a radio or handheld flare to get their attention. You can also signal with a small mirror.

How to Create a Flotation Device with Your Clothes

You've fallen overboard with all your clothes on, but without your life jacket. You can be saved by the seat of your pants (or by other clothes you have on), if you remain calm.

1 **Tread water.**

Keep your head above water the entire time.

2 **Lighten your load.**

Kick off your shoes. Your shoes act as weights and will drag you down. Remove any jewelry or other heavy items.

3 **If you are wearing pants . . .**

Wriggle out of them and tie each leg shut with a knot. Holding the waistband open, whip the pants over your head from back to front into the water. Once air is trapped inside, tie off the waistband using a belt or hold it closed with your hands. Lean on the inflated pants and float.

4. If you have a sundress, tank top, or tote bag . . .

Tie off the ends so air becomes trapped inside to make any of these items into a personal flotation device.

5. Refill the air every ten minutes.

To do this, untie one opening and wave the item over your head again.

ABOUT THE CONTRIBUTORS

AUTHORS

Alexander Lurie is a pseudonym for two book-publishing professionals who live in New York and New Jersey.

David Borgenicht is the co-author of all the books in the "Worst-Case Scenario" series. He lives in Philadelphia.

CONSULTANT

Mike Perham started sailing at six years old. At fourteen, he became the youngest person to sail solo across the Atlantic, a record that remains to this day. At sixteen he completed a record-breaking round-the-world solo voyage. He lives in England.

ILLUSTRATOR

Yancey Labat got his start with Marvel Comics and has since been illustrating children's books. He lives in New York.